upside

A world turne

The 1,000 year history of The Saints

MARK BRADFORD

This is a work of fiction. Names, characters, business, events and incidents are the products of the author's imagination. Any resemblance to actual persons, living or dead or yet to be born, or actual events past present and future is purely coincidental.

Printed in the United States of America
First Printing, 2021

Alchemy

ISBN-13: 978-1-7336622-5-3

markbradford.org

v1.3

DEDICATION

To fans of *The Sword and the Sunflower* duet, this book is dedicated to you and your curiosity.

And dear Ophelia.

ACKNOWLEDGEMENTS

You know who you are.

I acknowledge the paradox of a book that is written in chronological order but is best read after the fact.

upside down

The 1,000 year history of The Saints

A prequel to The Sword and the Sunflower duet.

THE MEETING

The smartly-dressed woman watched the visitors leave as they were escorted through the hallways under the conference room. The view below was perfect and allowed those in the room to observe those coming and going. The glass was tilted and tinted just so as to obscure the overseer from the observed, though rarely would those leaving think to glance upwards.

Watching visitors leave was a not only a favorite past time but it was considered the reward for spending time with those who would visit the company. She didn't like visitors much—even this group of three men and one woman.

The man standing beside her could not take his eyes off the group of four below as he spoke.

"I can't believe they met with us. Those are the most powerful and most recognized players in tech. You should have been down there with them walking them out."

His companion kept her slightly-narrowed eyes on them and smiled with her eyes. The dichotomy of the smiling eyes and the stern lips was unnerving to some. She chose not to reply. He continued as he glanced back and forth between her face and those below.

"Tell me you're amazed. Tell me you're at least stunned…?"

She continued staring but did indeed reply.

"You're right. They are the best. That woman was my idol growing up. Her creativity and strength were reminders to me that I could do it—that

I could not only run this, but make it more than my father ever hoped for. Those four influence and control what is essentially the technology of the world."

Her lack of emotion was now annoying her companion and it showed in his voice.

"Nikola. Nik. Tell me that you aren't impressed!?"

"Oh, I'm more than impressed."

"Finally." He relaxed as she turned her eyes on him. He smiled and sighed. "I can't believe you had a meeting with them, a summit. You got them to come here and…"

"Oh I'm not impressed by that."

He was forced to trail off as she had interjected matter-of-factly. Dumbfounded he inquired quietly.

"Then what are you impressed by?"

She focused her eyes on him. He could feel the confidence, and perhaps something else.

"That we don't need them at all."

INFINITE ENERGY SOLUTIONS

American Technology—the brainchild of Andrej Tesic—is rebranding as Infinite Energy Solutions, Inc. His daughter Nik Tesic has become the wunderkind of not only the technology world, but in matters related to energy. On the eve of the company filing its 200th patent, Ms. Tesic sat down with us to discuss her history, her father's passing and what is in store for IES—no pun intended. My interview with her is something of a dream come true for this reporter and it was not without its pitfalls. I can only describe the interview as something like being caught in an elevator with a dragon and it is forced to answer your mundane questions. To say I was both enamored and terrified is an understatement. I joined her at their corporate headquarters in Dallas, Texas.

Thank you for sitting down with us. Congratulations on your latest patent, and our condolences for the loss of your father.

Thank you.

Your father was a trail blazer in the realm of batteries and long-term storage, what was your thought process in rebranding?

I'm sure you've read all the insufferable media packages we've put out. My dad was brilliant and humble. I don't suffer from the latter personality defect. (laughs) So combining the additional new ip in our portfolio with a desire to expand it seemed only logical to rebrand. 'American Technology' was rather generic. 'Infinite Energy Solutions' was more accurate.

And 'infinite?' That's a tongue-in-cheek nod?

No. Not at all. Our understanding of energy is limited. Or rather, the other players in the field, globally are. We've come to understand that there's more to energy storage than a chemical reaction.

But infinite?

Yes. With the intense solarization of the planet and the conversion of everything to electrical, batteries in the traditional sense are by far the weakest link. It's what we worked on first—the storage of this energy—before we expanded into how to obtain it. But now we are on the cusp. Which is why we are talking. Imagine a water wheel in a fast-flowing river. You generate power from this. One could say that energy is never-ending and infinite. Sure the earth spins, gravity plays a part, condensation and the circle of weather continues to replenish the river, but to you it is an infinite power source.

A paradigm shift?

I hate that term.

What would you call it then? (laughs)

What do you call it when the caveman witnesses lightning and then figures out how to start his own fire? We've witnessed lightning for some time. I've figured out how to start the fire.

And when is that? The starting of the…

Shortly.

Let's talk about the accelerator.

Go on.

Your company's acquisition of the largest accelerator in the world came as a surprise to the technology community. The challenges your company faced were nothing short of monumental.

As had been reported, the five billion that was sunk into it was wasted. It was abandoned for all intents and purposes, and the chemical company that perched there for a few years did nothing with it. It was in line with our ip and a tool we needed for further advancement.

You've been very gracious in sharing your data with the scientific community.

Of course.

But there are those that say not *all* the data has been released.

We are allowed to keep whatever data we deem as proprietary information. Trade secrets.

If I may change gears with you.

By all means.

Your name—would you mind explaining its origin once and for all?

There is not much to explain. Nicola is a common girl's name on my country. My father favored the 'k.' That's it. Maybe he wanted a boy?

* Read the full interview in this weeks Titans of Tech. *

Nikola had already read through the unedited interview, as she was allowed to approve it before going to print. Listening to Stan read it aloud in her office allowed her to absorb it through his inflection. This habit made him nervous. It seemed inefficient.

Finally she spoke.

"Meh. It's a good article. It did what it was supposed to."

"'Moody and unpredictable, sometimes short.'"

Stan read the excepts of the review of the interview as she smiled.

"Thank you. Guilty as charged."

"I think you could have explained a bit more about our direction. Maybe? A few crumbs on the process? The massive cost of rebranding and when we would be finished? The reporter was eating up everything you said. He just wanted a bit more human interest I think."

He tried to soften the blow of his suggestion. It would not have made a difference. She was no-nonsense. He would never become accustomed to that.

"No. I was there to assert our dominance in the field, to explain our direction minimally without revealing our hand, and to allude to our newest tech. The latter is what got us this meeting."

"And, um, what was the purpose of the meeting?"

"To make sure no one else could start the fire."

"And…?"

"They can't."

"Oh."

Nikola smiled and grabbed a small square from her pocket. Stan recognized the small foldable device. She slapped it onto the table—far harder than he was comfortable with. She was unapologetic about being rough with electronics which was directly the opposite of what he'd expect of one of the leading engineers in the world. She spoke two words.

"Two years."

He looked at the device, then up at her.

"OK? Um…"

"Two years yesterday. It would have been cooler if it would have coincided with the meeting today, but that's as close as we could get the meeting."

"Wait, you arranged the meeting date so that it lined up with…"

"Almost."

"I don't understand. What is two years…"

She flipped it open to show the glowing screen. It looked like a normal personal device. Turning it in her hand with admiration in her voice she explained.

"The battery. Two years. It's been running constantly. No fluctuations, no reduction within acceptable parameters."

Then Stan understood.

"You took it out of the building!? Nik. How could you… It hasn't been approved for… Isn't that dangerous? You've been carrying that *on your person*?! If the authorities found out..?"

He was exasperated, confused, and seemed afraid.

"A pinhole."

He shook his head and couldn't find common ground. And her two-word sentences didn't help.

"You mean it's that small. That doesn't make it any less dangerous that you are taking a ball of energy outside of the lab. Oh my god did you travel with it? Did you put this through security scans out there in the air…"

"No, not a ball—a hole. A hole in the shape of a ball."

"I… I don't know how that is relevant. What difference does that make?"

"Stan, you're almost shaking."

He took a breath and composed himself. He was yelling at his boss and arguably the most powerful woman in the world, and the most powerful engineer in the world bar none. And she seemed to be enjoying it. He knew she shared things with him that she'd never share with others. He had something that no one else had—her trust. To him it was more valuable than anything else, but this was reckless. She had quietly taken an experimental energy source outside of the building for no less than two years. There was no telling how many countless people she had exposed to danger. And she just carried it on her person like it was an extended-life battery.

She continued as his composure returned.

"Of course it is relevant. It's a hole in something we didn't know you could make a hole in. It's free energy. And it's containable—clearly. And this is just a pinhole. A pinhole Stan!"

She put the device back on the table and he stared at the screen.

"Even with the containment area it still fits in this. And that pinhole produces enough to run ten of these easily."

She smiled at him and her eyes said 'I have a secret.'

"Nik? What are you planning? What are you…?"

"We open tomorrow. I've moved the date back."

Stan had long understood that his boss' way of expressing time was backwards to others. Moving something *back* meant changing it to an *earlier* date. She was referring to the big test. They meant to run the accelerator.

"Tomorrow?"

"Yes."

"But the cloud? Social? I've mad no arrangements for them to be there, or us to stream. They've asked almost daily about a firm date. They will not be happy about hearing about it after the fact."

Then he realized something else.

"Do we have approval of this test?"

"There's no danger, thus no approval."

His eyes widened as he stared at her device.

"Oh Stan. We can ask forgiveness afterwards. At that time we will have created the greatest energy source the world has ever seen. Pure, unending power for everything. 'Sustainable' will lose meaning. This is beyond sustainable. This is for all intents and purposes, *infinite*."

For months he had fielded messages and calls from the media. He had answered questions she refused to even acknowledge. Protests were dampened, fears were assuaged and queries were half answered. Most of his effort was spent on damage control and prevention—yet she barely seemed to care. Why was that? Was it that he bore the emotional burden of it all while she just executed her plans?

The screen of the device on the table stared back at him in contempt.

THE REPORTER

"Word in the cloud is that she'll do this any time now, but most likely in the next few months—certainly by the end of the year."

Martin listened to the female voice in his ear advise him accordingly. His friend and fellow journalist was almost as eager to get the story as he was, but her information was outdated.

"Carly. I don't think so."

He adjusted his pant leg in the car as he spoke. The driver zipped him along at a pace a bit faster than he would like so he almost bumped his head on the seat in front of him in the process. He grimaced at the driver.

"What? You don't think so? Ok, smart guy, you tell me then."

He smiled a huge smile and it was wasted as the driver continued to look forward. Realizing she couldn't see it either, he spoke.

"I'll tell you tomorrow. I promise. In fact I think I may want to have drinks."

"Have drinks? You? You taking a break? You getting married? Martin…"

Her voice turned uncharacteristically serious.

"You *OK*?"

He laughed and the sound put her at ease.

"Yes of course! I didn't know you cared?"

"Fuck you. Call me when you have more info or you post, cool?"

"Yeah. Kisses."

He tapped his earpiece and tried to remain calm. The text had come out of no where and he half-believed it. If it hadn't come from so high up he wouldn't have even considered it. But here he was, on his way to the most recognizable company in the country, for an audience with its CEO and exclusive access to those conducting the most anticipated experiment in modern history.

Now if the guards didn't stop him he'd know it was all real.

—

The security procedures for IES were intentionally overcomplicated for first-time visitors and those that were not part of the company. Those that gained the trust of Nikola were eventually upgraded to a simpler—but equally intrusive—procedure.

Martin was currently going through the aforementioned overcomplicated procedure and his eyes and mouth hurt. The former from the amount of reflexive eye rolling and the latter because he could not lose the grin. With every step he was closer to the inner circle. It was an arduous journey of repetitive checks and searches and pauses but one thing had gotten him farther and farther: the name of the man that had summoned him.

Unlike his boss, the man that had summoned him chose to welcome his visitors in person.

"Martin. You made it."

The reporter continued to smile as he put himself back together—refilling his pockets, zipping up his pack and resetting his footwear.

"I told you to keep your goodies to a minimum."

"Sorry. I know! You said 'more goodies mean more time in security.'"

He continued to smile and noticed his host looked a little nervous. Having never met in person he was unsure if this was just a personality quirk or if he actually was. This was a planned meeting and the reporter sure should be the anxious one. Yet Stan was practically looking over his shoulder. But for what, or whom?

They shook hands and Stan guided them to an elevator which swiftly carried them to their destination—a small conference room on the top floor. Martin had heard about the flourishes on the building. There were elevators with one destination and entire floors that were just one room. In a way it was like a medieval castle with secret observation areas and even passageways.

At least that was the rumor.

A flat, single-use manufacturing building with a few offices this was not.

Martin was glad to have the chance to meet Nikola, as her recent interview was the only time she'd spoken to the press directly. This would be exciting even with Stan there as her handler. Perhaps it would go smoothly because of that.

Stan spoke immediately in serious tones which set the mood.

"Nikola will not be joining us."

"Oh. Ok."

The pregnant pause was uncomfortable. At last his host spoke again.

"In fact, she doesn't know I invited you."

Martin's eyebrows raced up his head in response as he replied.

"She doesn't? I mean, well, I'm sure she is busy organizing and managing the experiment and the presentation, as well as the other media, the cloud and so forth, right?"

"No. I mean, she, well, she didn't invite *any* media. She didn't want any media and this test is supposed to be reported after the fact."

"But you invited me?"

Martin was at once honored and confused, and was starting to feel like he'd been set up—ever so slightly. Still, it was the story of a lifetime, and he could parley it into something amazing, regardless.

"Yes, I did Martin. I appreciate your work and you've always been fair with us."

"Well, I appreciate that, sir. I would like to think I write with integrity. It is something that is sorely lacking in the media these days and what not only sets…"

Stan waved the response away. Martin's answers were entirely too long and mostly pre-prepared. He didn't have the time for an in-depth discussion on ethics.

"I need you to be here. I need someone to be here."

Martin interjected quickly.

"Is this on the record?"

Stan looked annoyed, and Martin was starting to think anxiety was a natural state for the man.

"The what? No. Yes. Look, I don't care. I need someone to be here for this. It's bigger than my job. Look—Nikola is brilliant. But sometimes she's blinded by her own logic. She's never been wrong. But maybe that's today. I don't know."

"And that's why you wanted me here? As an outside observer, or a reporter?"

"Yes, a bit of both."

"Go *wrong*?"

Again there was a pause and the air between them felt thick. Stan leaned into the beautiful and comically large conference table. Only a chair separated them but the two men still seemed far from each other. The room absorbed the sound they made and would not return it to their ears. His host spoke in grave terms.

"I know I am putting you on the spot. If everything goes well you will have an exclusive story and I will deal with Nikola—if I still have a job. But if things don't go well you can be an independent conduit to the world."

Martin swallowed. All humor, prepared statements and bravado had drained from him now.

"What could go wrong? I didn't know this was a dangerous experiment? I thought you were just officially doing the big energy experiment? The reactor has been on line for some time now. I've read about the data you provide."

Stan shrugged. He was right and his calm statement almost made him feel better.

"Yes of course. You are most probably right and there is nothing to worry about."

"Am… am I in danger?"

"What? You mean from the device? The building? Oh no. No."

Martin tilted his head like a dog hearing a distant siren.

"Then why the caution? You seem worried."

"I am."

His responses weren't helping the confusion. Martin tried a direct, firm route. He was already here and this conversation alone was gold.

"Ok, you need to be straight with me right now."

He placed his hand on the table and allowed each finger to support his arm—like a spider—as he continued. It was the reporter's power move and he had gotten much flak from his friend for it. He spoke in serious tones.

"What exactly is going on here? What are you afraid of and most importantly what *exactly* shook you so much that you involved me in this way? You are putting me in a difficult situation."

It was confidently said. Stan's confidence in the man was validated. He responded in kind.

"The experiment today was supposed to be the big reveal in an energy experiment that would produce an energy source that is seemingly infinite. It is a repeat of something we did a long time ago."

"A test?"

"No, apparently it wasn't a test and it produced an energy source—but a tiny one. This is going to be a big one. It is not a showy test for the media. It is the actual procedure that will produce the energy source again."

"OK… but…"

"This time it will be ten thousand times larger."

"Thats… that's not a test."

Boy you people don't play fucking games. No middle ground for you.

"No, we are skipping any intermediary tests. Nikola is convinced it's just numbers. A tiny bit was good, much more is awesome."

"That's reckless."

Stan pushed his lips together into a thin line.

"Now you know why you're here."

Stan sat back into his chair. His burden was released. The reporter absorbed what he could and fired off rapid questions.

"Well… Where am I going to be standing? You and I are going to drive down to the accelerator together? I can take all of my equip… won't your boss kick me out if she sees me? Even before I can…"

Stan sat back up. So much for the burden being lifted.

"*Martin.* You will be embedded with a group of engineers. No, your equipment will not be permitted there and…"

"Well how am I going to…"

"The procedure and the entire area is recorded on many levels and you'll be given access to the files."

Martin was unconvinced. Stan continued.

"You understand there is no way I can just let you appear there?

Effectively I am sneaking you in as a junior engineer. If you think the procedure for visitors to this building is stringent you have no idea on the cleansing the engineers go through for these kinds of procedures."

Martin flashed the next 24 hours though his mind. The possibilities, the files, the report. He was immune to any prosecution at this point. He would have his story, his files and his host would most likely suffer the consequences because of his paranoia. Though it seemed on the surface to be a dangerous thing in reality this was just a chance of a lifetime. His career would truly start tomorrow.

His friend would definitely be buying him a drink. He summed all those thoughts up in four words.

"When do we leave?"

THE DOOR OPENS

The facility was less than an hour drive from the IES headquarters in Dallas. It seemed rather serendipitous to have established said headquarters so close to the only machine in the world capable of properly serving the needs of their business. Martin made a mental note to research any connections between the two. Perhaps he'd even find something unscrupulous dating five decades back, perhaps not. He decided in an instant it wasn't worth pursuing at this point as his plate was not only full but overflowing—metaphorically speaking. He had enough to report on moving forward.

True to his word Stan had done an excellent job setting him up with credentials as a junior engineer. In his case he was an intern with the same name. It seemed that once workers had passed muster they were relatively unmolested and watched as long as they followed the rules. With this guise he was added to a group of engineers on their way to the facility. There wasn't much small talk in the short ride and he was grateful for it. Having never done an undercover report he found the whole thing rather exciting.

The car passed through the gate and onto the facility. As a group they exited and made their way to their stations. In this case it was a small room of screens with an actual window looking upon the front of the machine.

After their meeting Martin had returned to his office and done as much research as possible on the accelerator. He viewed all the images he could of the facility both in and out. Being a generalist, his technical aptitude wasn't on par with his fellow tech reporters, but his willingness to learn and look at the big picture more than made up for it.

The facility matched what he'd seen, and he understood that the vast majority of the machine was underground and many miles long. Accelerators were typically just a huge underground tunnel that was in the shape of a ring. The attachments and protrusions shown in the images made it look like an old sci-fi prop with wires and cylinders coming out of it at odd angles. The ring of the machine was completely enclosed but a tunnel on the outside of the ring allowed engineers to maintain and adjust it—by means of things resembling golf carts. No one wanted to walk for miles in the tunnel to reach the point of interest.

Speaking of which, his final stop for the day was the mouth of the device. Typically machines of this nature had no such mouth but apparently Nikola's procedure involved an additional piece of equipment affixed and embedded into what was commonly known as the 'front' of the ring.

The scientific community was aware of it and Martin had watched more than one video on a scientist or would-be scientist theorize exactly what such a device would do. Some even thought it was an elaborate ruse to throw off the competition.

But this was exactly the focus of today's visit.

Martin was amazed at how little conversation was had between the group of engineers and the workers at the facility. They seemed almost solemn. Perhaps they knew the gravity of the situation? Perhaps they too shared his host's fears? Most likely it was the engineer mindset—people committed to technology tended to be introverts focused mainly on their work. Regardless, he was very grateful—all the prepared conversations and knowledge of the facility probably wouldn't be used. He may very well be able to do his job in silence and leave by stealth.

"Graves. Here."

His superior for the day grunted to him and pointed.

Martin moved quickly to what appeared to be his station. As an intern he was merely there to observe, which was exactly what he was there for as a reporter.

He moved quickly into place and smiled a bit. The man that shouted eyed him up closely and for a second he panicked. Though he was a behind-the-scenes reporter his face was still on his articles. Was he recognized? The man stared intently.

"When it blows up make sure you don't drop your pad."

Martin stared into the man's brown eyes. Apparently his fear and confusion were well placed. The man broke into a smile and clapped him on his back.

"Just observe everything you can. And stay in your space here."

Martin smiled a weak smile and felt enormous relief as he watched the man exit the small room.

He truly had a front row seat to the proceedings. The large oval was upright and just twenty feet or so behind the observation window. It looked like a vault door without the door—just an opening with darkness and metal. But what treasure lie inside? He almost guffawed at the sentences he was constructing for his article. The corny title was in the running right now.

That's when he saw her.

The blonde woman in a very expensive—yet subdued—grayish-blue suit appeared out of no where to walk in front of the door. She spoke to one of the technicians milling about and touched various locations on the perimeter of the opening. She seemed almost like a director making sure the props were secured just before the performance. He wondered what might have been different if the press had been officially allowed to attend. He mused that he would have removed some of the engineers and added a bit of lighting as the center of attention was a bit dark. At that very thought the room he viewed suddenly lit up. Startled, he looked over at others. A taller man smiled and said simply, "I wish they would keep it untinted and just let us wear glasses."

"Uh huh"

The grunt was all Martin could muster as he watched the room darken a bit—this time understanding that the entire window was tinted automatically. Apparently the show was going to get bright.

He followed the woman with fascination. Her hair was in a bob cut and she seemed absolutely in control. He recognized her as Nikola and for the first time he was intimidated. He was also thankful that the window was once again tinted and assumed it worked both ways. Feeling his heart pounding rapidly he wondered if he should just wander over to the side of the room, but he did not want to give up his perfect viewing position. Hopefully she would be done shortly and the show would start without him being discovered. Worst case scenario was throwing Stan under the bus, metaphorically. And yet he was actually frightened. He continued to watch her as he took emotional inventory. That was all he could do as he waited.

Fortunately he didn't have to wait long.

—

There was little to be found on line as to exactly how running a collider would occur. There were no giant switches but instead rather tame monitors in place—most of them touch-sensitive in lieu of another input device. A large rotating warning light came to life. In fact, there were number of them in the chamber he was viewing. He could see that there must be many of them in the ring-shaped corridor that went off into the distance. Each one came to life lightly and started spinning. It was the kind of thing used decades ago, and was an interesting touch that IES never upgraded them to something more electronic and not mechanical.

It did a great job adding to his anxiety.

A cart and driver emerged from the tunnel to the right. The cart was parked and everyone left the room. There was no countdown that he was aware of, but he was fairly sure that the main controls were upstairs in the large room he'd passed through—the one that reminded him of NASA.

But she was still there. She had only stepped out of his view and returned. She stood less than twenty feet from the large opening. Surely she was going to leave the room before it was turned on?

Martin had come across a story of a man who had literally stuck his head in an operating accelerator, or rather it had been turned on while he was fixing it. The man lost hearing and some of the initial results were gruesome. Apparently he survived and continued his work after some damage had occurred. Was this different? This was the outside anyway. But what was with the opening? Opening to what? Did she just slap a hole onto it? Maybe it was an additional viewing window.

He was afraid for her. What was it he'd called her?

Reckless.

She folded her hands together, like a daughter waiting for her father to pick her up from school. It was the first vulnerability he'd seen in this woman.

He could hear it now. Well, he thought he could hear it but after a few seconds he realized he could feel it. It was a sound in the ears that seemed to be nowhere and everywhere—not static electricity but something entirely different.

The glass was even darker now and some of his group were whispering. This event was obviously something that every engineer in the company would have fought to be a part of—and here he was.

As she was off to the side, at his angle he could see half of her face and even through the now-dimmed glass he thought he saw her mouth move. She said three words.

That was when it happened. There was no sound or warning but he would swear later than he thought it blew her hair back when it appeared.

It was a ball of energy the exact dimensions of the hole—more oval than round, taller than wider. The color was white and blue and vivid. It was the best special effect he'd ever seen up close that wasn't. Even through the filter it was still a very bright and impressive thing. It did not throb, or pulse or ungulate; it was rock solid and just was. The light lit up her face and her suit—which he realized was remarkably like the color of the thing, as if she had dressed accordingly.

The men and women in his room gasped, and did not exhale. Then they all clapped and some of them even hugged. He imagined the same thing was going on in the control room upstairs. He was right. He could feel the positive energy in the room along with the indescribable sound-that-was-energy.

As the glass became clear again he saw her turn away and thought he saw something on her face catch the light more than her skin—a tear.

Just then he realized he wasn't sure what to do. Was this it? A big ball shows up and then he gets all the video from the records and the security cams? This was best case scenario. Stan wouldn't be fired, nothing horrible would happen and he'd have the story of the decade.

As it turned out he as wrong on all accounts.

UPSIDE DOWN

The entire encounter seemed as if he was in a dream. It had been so easy to be embedded in the group, and so easy to return to corporate. He assumed that he'd just meet with Stan and be handed a storage device? Or would his files be waiting in the cloud. He felt more like a spy who had completed his mission save for the final reward. Though it seemed like hours he went with the flow of his group and made his way outside of the building. He did not see Nikola or any security guards rushing him. He made it.

There was a problem with the car, however. The driver was unable to start it. He could engage it, but it would not allow him to be on his way.

"What's up…?"

Yeah, that sounded normal.

"Uh, the GPS won't lock."

The driver was confused and annoyed and he spoke to the car.

"I know where I'm going. I don't need GPS!"

He eventually found a way to override it and they were on their way. This of course started a conversation between all of the engineers in the vehicle. The pent up excitement was turned into over-the-top troubleshooting regarding why and how the car wouldn't drive. He sat back and listened and nodded when appropriate. In the half-hour drive it was discovered that it was the compass. The car's GPS was fine, but it had to wait to rely solely on it. The compass, however, could no longer find north. Now that everyone's device had been returned to them they experimentally took them out. Every device and watch and ring could not find north reliably.

There had been chatter about the Earth's poles shifting for some time. In fact, magnetic north had shifted years ago and was supposedly dancing around in Europe. The poles had theoretically shifted every 300,000 and perhaps it would happen any year now. This was said year after year and they'd predicted by now that it would shift. Years ago it had started a mild panic until the general populace found something more interesting focus on—like the latest pop song. Perhaps it had finally jumped?

The Texas summer was particularly hot this day and he stared through the sunroof at the clouds to clear his mind from all the chatter. It was like listening to five science channels at once and his brain hurt.

It didn't help that the sunroof on this car had a weird purple tint to it which made the sky look unnatural.

He was no stranger to Texas traffic but what he saw made his heart sink: it was bumper to bumper traffic for as far as he could see. The driver slammed on the breaks and turned the car off.

"What the hell?"

Martin was irritated and at his wits end. It was a rookie move for the driver to just panic like that. He'd been in traffic all the time and there was never a need to shut down a car that was drawing minimal power just sitting there. Screens took nothing compared to the motors, and he assumed the driver had ample battery left.

"I… it wasn't me."

The driver took his hands off the wheel and held his palms up to accentuate his innocence.

The front passenger jabbed at the dark screen and the grabbed the wheel —much to the irritation of the diver. Just then the screen came on, and promptly winked off again.

Martin realized that he saw no break lights ahead. Either everyone had just parked their cars or their car was experiencing what they all were.

"Oh that's not good. It won't come up."

This time it was the woman next to him. She held her device in hand and shook her watch. She tapped both repeatedly and tried any and all buttons that were visible. Her devices—like everyone's in the car—were dead.

Much to his dismay this started the chatter again.

Again he was listening to five separate troubleshooting broadcasts that he could not tune out.

"Open a window."

"I can't"

Martin got out of the car into the heat before his fellow passenger ever had a chance to ask him to move. The ride was becoming stuffy and overwhelming and he couldn't help himself.

He squinted to see the cars up ahead. People were scattered on the highway. Some were standing and some were pacing.

And some were looking up. Martin joined them and he felt his mouth fall open.

It wasn't the sunroof; the sky actually had a slight purple tint to it. He was at least relieved that the heat he expected would greet him was absent. In fact it was rather tolerable for a 95 degree day. He couldn't imagine what it would be like to exit the car and stand out in 100 degree weather while all the gasoline cars pumped hot exhaust at him. To him it felt more like 70. There was a cool breeze and he still couldn't shake the feeling of a ringing in his ears with no sound. He opened his mouth a few times to pop his ears. It didn't help.

His compatriots were in a heated discussion as to the cause. He turned to them nonchalantly and in a confident voice yelled into the group.

"You think it was the experiment?"

They all froze and turned to him. They stared.

At least two of them wrinkled their noses and squinted at the prospect.

"The what? The procedure? No! Of course not."

The woman chimed in.

"Who *are* you anyway?"

Martin turned back to the sky and spoke without looking at them.

"I think I'm the guy that was supposed to be here."

—

Eventually the group made their way on the highway on foot and joined the crowd of people walking to the city. Corporate was only two miles away or so—they guessed. There was much chatter about their homes, where they were from, and what was happening there.

"Do you think she's still back there? Or maybe she made it to corporate?"

"Who?"

"Ms. Tesic."

"Maybe she's out there in that crowd?"

The man pointed to the mass of cars and people ahead.

Martin listened in silence and walked along with the group. He wanted to call his friend and check in, and reach out to his sister in New York. That wasn't possible as there was still no way to communicate. The engineers were very specific about the electronics fail.

"Its *Eeyem.*"

Martin turned to the engineer that spoke gibberish.

"Huh? What's 'eeyem?'"

The man stopped walking and stared at Martin.

"E. M. An e. m. pulse."

"What?"

The man continued in annoyed tones and spoke to Martin as if he was a child. In this matter he was.

"EM. Electromagnetic Pulse. They used to have bombs that did that. All electronics give off a little radiation. You know; why you are supposed to turn your devices off on a plane. If you create a super-strong pulse it disables electronics temporarily."

The woman shook her head and interjected.

"Yeah, but you can't generate a pulse of that strength dude."

"Yes you can."

"Theoretically, but you still have to blow something up. Or explode a nuclear bomb in the sky."

Martin looked back up at the slightly-purplish clouds and spoke.

"Wouldn't we have seen that? Is that why… um… the sky is *purple*?"

"What about the sun? A coronal mass ejection could do this. It *did* do this a long time…"

"The Carrington event."

"Yeah"

Martin again looked confused and this time they were happy to teach him.

"The Carrington event happened about 200 years ago. The sun threw off some plasma. A solar storm. The sun does this all the time. But this was a particularly strong burst and it was pointed right at the Earth."

They all were nodding, and taking turns.

"Telegraph operators got zapped with the electricity the lines picked up. There were no electronics back then, but if there were they would have been fried."

"We protect against that now. We fortify electronics to be heartier. The tensions with China a few decades ago caused people in our industry to think harder about protection."

The woman grabbed her device and shoved it in Martin's direction like it was a dead fish.

"Our stuff was supposed to withstand that. Easily."

Martin considered it all, and did his best to follow. All of his equipment was back at corporate. He summarized as it was part of his job.

"So you guys think that a foreign nation exploded a nuclear bomb in the sky and it made some sort of electro… electromagnetic pulse that fried the electronics in *everything*?"

There was a pause and in the silence Martin continued. He was suddenly terrified.

"*Jesus!* Are we in a fallout area? What about radiation poisoning? Wait, what about the experiment back there?!"

"We told you that's not the kind of energy the procedure creates."

Martin clicked his tongue at how sure the engineer seemed. He corrected him.

"No, I mean what about all the electronics and stuff that make it go and…"

"The containment field…"

The engineer that interjected had done so with a dreamy look in his eyes.

"What. *What* containment field!?"

Martin was getting irate at all the prospects. That this simple thing could cause so much harm was insane.

What a fucking Achilles heel. Why does nobody talk about this?

Everything was based on sensitive electronics—from his toaster to his car. Even his electric razor. He wondered why a superpower had never used it before. He was convinced they just did. But what about the experiment? It was all too coincidental. The compass, the pulse, the experiment—they all happened at the same time.

Again he tried to make sense of it all.

“OK, so if the sun decided to squirt us with stuff that caused these kind of catastrophic results, wouldn’t we get a warning? Don’t we have some sort of monitoring system? Haven’t we somehow shielded electronics against this?”

Once again they took turns answering. He didn’t remember who was saying what, just that someone was talking. To him the group was one big answer box.

“We wouldn’t get much of a warning. Eight minutes. The sun is only eight minutes away by light. And this stuff travels at a rate that can just take hours or even a day or so.”

“Yes, we fortify our electronics. Our company standards for it are five times that of what is common. Tesic insists on it.”

Martin nodded and replied to his answer box.

“OK, so you guys think it's *not* an attack? Most likely its this Carrington thing happening again? I don’t have to worry about radiation? And like we’re done for another 200 years?”

“Yeah, that’s what we think.”

Martin took a breath. The group had stopped to have the question and answer session. He felt slightly better after the conversation. Things would return back to normal. It was a … what was it called again? A ‘coronal mass ejection.’ Yeah. So much to write about. So weird not to have anything to record with. He didn’t even have a pad and pen. Well, a physical pad and pen with paper and everything. He was starting to smile and enjoy the ride now.

That feeling would have continued had it not been for the horrible purple lightning that was now flashing in the distance.

It seemed a storm was approaching.

NIKOLA AND THE DOOR

"She's still standing there."

The staff of the collider facility had mostly emptied. Some were stuck in the parking lot, some were stuck in the control room and some decided to stay as part of their duties. Arthur was the lead engineer and VP of the collider facility. He stood in the viewing area and watched his boss as she stood next to the massive glowing oval.

He spoke to his assistant who flanked him in the small room. She seemed frightened; Nikola did not. His boss had a dreamy look on her face as she stared at the light.

The window had failsafes and all systems in the building had not only backup generators but specialized backup batteries created by IES. None of that was working—including the auto-tinting mechanism on the window—so he could see her quite clearly alongside the bright light.

Her blue eyes took on an almost angelic appearance as the light blended quite well with the natural color. She seemed like she was in a trance.

"Have you seen the sky?"

His assistant inquired timidly as they both stared at the lone subject in the room.

"No. The sky? What do you mean?"

"It's purple."

He blinked and took his eyes off of his boss.

"*Purple*?"

He said the word as if it was made up. Surely now wasn't the time to panic and make bizarre associations between the procedure and natural occurrences. He'd had more than his fill of doomsayers and those that said the world would end the first time they ran this collider. They'd said it in the past for other colliders too.

Of course this was quite different than smashing one particle into another and examining the aftermath. He knew full well how different.

"What's the status of the facility. Is *anything* working yet?"

His assistant looked back at the oval. Instead of answering she asked a question.

"How is that still able to form? None of the equipment is powered. Shouldn't it collapse?"

Arthur's face changed to grim.

"I don't know. I suspect she may. When the power comes back on…"

"Sir I don't think it's just power."

"What do you mean?"

"We thought it was a surge. But now they think it is a pulse. The senior engineering staff believe it was an EM pulse."

"Well that's damn shitty timing then! Where did it come from? There are no flares expected. Though today wasn't the optimal timing for this procedure there wasn't any expected disturb…"

"From us."

Arthur paused at the interruption.

"What? Where? How?"

"From this building, or somewhere very near. We are the epicenter."

The older man moved to the door and with some difficulty was able to manually force it to open. And least that worked.

Quickly he was at Nikola's side.

He looked at the giant oval of energy, then to her. It was a frightening thing. He had seen the smaller manifestation and been part of the small group that conducted the first procedure—and sworn to secrecy with the others.

Now he looked at the bright thing with fear.

"Nik. Nik. We should leave here."

"We did it."

Her response was slow, and she acted as if intoxicated.

"You have to leave this room. There no telling what…"

She blinked and lost some of her sluggishness.

"No telling? Of course there is this 'telling' Arthur. We know exactly what this is and what it is emitting."

"Well then we should leave anyway Nik."

He grabbed her shoulder to spin her away from it.

"There have been developments. Something else has happened."

She blinked again, and looked like she'd just woken up.

"What? Arthur?"

She touched his arm and for the first time moved away.

"Come with me please."

—

"It's stuffy in here. Why isn't the AC working? Why isn't the power on? The backups? We are a power company and we have no power!?"

Arthur had never heard his boss yell. Her demeanor was always stern, matter-of-fact and collected. Her words were final to the point that they didn't need to be loud. But she was different now—as if just waking from a dream. It reminded him of an unfortunate soul who slept past their alarm and showed up to work straight from their bed.

“We seem to have created a problem, Ms. Tesic. There…”

She cut him off. She needed questions answered, and was irritated by the feeling of having lost some time.

“Arthur, you are in charge of this facility. I want my questions answered, in order, now. Then you’re going to explain quickly what you mean by ‘creating a problem.’ And in the mean time your staff is going to get the AC back on.”

He took a deep breath. It wasn’t the first time he’d seen her make a request of someone who didn’t answer her questions. He knew it. He fell in the trap he’d managed to avoid for over five years. Hopefully he remembered them all, in order.

“The AC isn’t working because all equipment is offline. There is no power to anything that we know at this time.”

Her eyes widened and she almost interjected, but held her words to see if he could continue with all the answers. He cleared his throat.

“We believe because of an EM pulse there has been cascade failure of all electronics—and yes, even though they are heavily fortified against that sort of thing and yes even though we fortify many times industry standard.”

“*Military*. Go on.”

“Because of the failure the generators are non-functional. The panels, the batteries—none of them function. It is an EM pulse unlike we have ever seen. The only thing close to it…”

“A solar flare? A fucking solar flare Arthur?”

“You… you moved the procedure.”

“What?! Oh come on. You think we’re that unlucky that a freak solar flare hits today? You are blaming me, no?”

His eyes widened.

"No of course not I'm just saying that…"

She looked for her device while he apologized.

"Ms. Tesic *nothing* works. It's not even about the power, it's about the electronics—the tech."

She shook her head in disbelief. He was wrong. A flare of this magnitude was not expected for decades. She was ahead of everyone in the fortification of her sensitive electronics and…

"Why is that still open?!"

She spoke so quickly that Arthur almost jumped. Her head had rotated towards the oval and the question was shouted at the window.

"Nik?"

"If the electronics all failed, if we have no power, how is that still open? I know it draws power from itself and is self-sustaining but those are very sensitive electronics."

She sped out of the room and right up to the semi-sphere. He watched in fear as she ran her hand around the metal ring that surrounded it. She took a step back and looked back at him with her palms raised upwards. She didn't know. She always knew.

That was when the orb flashed brighter for a second. She turned her head back to it. Having her stand so close to it made him very nervous. He knew that whatever energy came from it was nothing physics had explained so far—it wasn't electricity or heat, or even radiation as they knew it. She had found a way to harness the unusual energy and turn it into something they could use. She'd essentially created a converter to generate electricity, so there should be no danger standing right next to it.

And he was the only person aware of what powered her personal device.

But now it was open, nothing supported it, and it showed no signs of closing.

At least it wasn't getting any larger.

The orb pulsed again.

"Get in here!"

He yelled to her and knocked his fist on the glass.

It pulsed again. And then again.

"Nik!"

She took a step back as it pulsed three more times. He saw that she was squinting to look into it—as if she'd seen something. His palms were pressed onto the glass as he waited for the inevitable.

MARTIN'S RETURN

Still thankful for the odd reprieve from the heat, Martin and his group continued their walk towards downtown. The highway they were on was surrounded by green, and cement led the way forward and back. He was also grateful for Stan having the forethought to embed him with a group of people who probably had more answers to what happened than anyone within hundreds of miles. Granted, they weren't NASA scientists, but they were junior engineers at IES and that made them the best of the best out there. There were only a few companies with the quality standards in employees that equaled Infinite Storage Solutions. And these people would answer any question he had.

More than once sparks flew from a small assortment of cars. It happened numerous times, as if they knew to take turns erupting. More than once a personal device on their persons also erupted. Once someone screamed at the heat generated and tossed their device to the ground. Any technology they carried had been thoroughly and irrevocably destroyed.

It seemed the pulses were getting stronger. Whatever disrupted the cars to begin with was now strong enough to destroy their electronics. Each pulse enforced this on the poor machines. The engineers explained to Martin that the charged particles were inadvertently collected by the wires and such and had nowhere else to go so erupted with a mini lightning storm. Parts were fused together. There was no telling how many burns had been suffered by the population who carried a device, a watch, a ring—anything that could conduct this electricity that was now ever-present.

Hospitals. Oh dear God.

The same was happening with the sky. Fortunately the lightning he'd seen so far was only cloud to cloud. He had no idea what purple lightning would do it it struck the ground, or a building.

The group assured Martin that seeking shelter was useless, and that until they saw cloud to ground lightning they wouldn't be any less safe in the crowd. His heart sunk at the discussion of electronics in the area, the country and perhaps even the world. This made the Carrington event like the static shock one gets from a carpet.

Was there nothing left though? How extensive was this? His mind raced and he just focused on his destination. For now it was IES corporate. They would have the most answers, and despite what his entourage affirmed he thought they were the cause.

They fell to silence as the continued their journey with the group of disgruntled, terrified motorists who were now on foot. It was surreal and some even spoke of the rapture. Whatever flavor of your religion, it was time for many to play the end of days card.

It was interesting to see what would generate chatter again and he didn't have to wait long.

It manifested in the form of a car up ahead.

The tail lights were blinking. The owner had obviously tried turning them on before exiting.

A few of the group ahead had gathered around it. They were opening doors, manipulating controls. When he and the engineers caught up they pronounced it fully functional. In fact, they could drive it away if it wasn't for it being entirely gridlocked. The owner was obviously long gone and part of the crowd ahead. He or she had most certainly been walking for hours and would have no knowledge of the functional auto.

He and the extended group marveled at it. He but had to glance at them to get an answer, or two, or three.

"Well, solar flares are rather complex. They aren't perfect spheres expanding outwards. They dance and bounce on the magnetic field of the Earth—and the environment plays a part on the effects."

"Yes, I bet the cars around it absorbed the brunt of it. Quite a fluke. Amazing that it is completely intact though. No damage at all."

"Sporadic."

"If you say so."

It was Martin. The more he listened, the more he thought they guessed. Maybe the difference between engineers and reporters was that the latter's guesses were more apparent. Upon reflection perhaps both were equal.

One more car was found to be functional, but this time it showed signs of serious damage. Some cars were smoking and some were on fire.

His compatriots—like a good portion of the crowd—were in tears. It was truly a nightmarish landscape. The purple lighting lit up the swirling clouds, the liminal space of a silent highway full of cars and people walking—the fires and the smoke—all contributed to a bad movie. Martin hoped for the third act to show up. His thoughts were of his sister, and his friend. There was no news, no way to contact others.

If they were lucky the flare had spared some critical components of the infrastructure up ahead. Perhaps the government had a contingency plan. He tried to cheer himself up with positive thoughts, but he didn't know what was worse—the great crying and terrified masses, or the solemnness of the engineers with him.

To his utter disappointment it was both.

He had no way to record his thoughts, or capture great video of the event. No news drones flew by; no planes made their appearance known. The worst indicator for him was that he saw no military whatsoever. Surely they were shielded from this—deep in some secret mountain installation.

"What about the satellites?"

He asked out of no where just to break his own train of thought.

"What? I guess it depends on the side of the…"

"No, no Tom, doesn't matter for the most part. If it did this then it's…"

"Are they going to fall out of the sky?!"

Martin's attempt to make himself distracted made things worse, it seemed, and he didn't mean to shout at them. At least he made them smile.

"No. Well, eventually. They all do that. We sometimes make them fall out. If they are small enough then they just burn up completely. Otherwise we have the remains splash down in the ocean."

Martin wasn't certain he liked the use of the word 'remains.'

Eventually they found themselves at IES corporate.

And it was in the middle of hell.

THE ARRIVAL

We are here.
We.
What is this.
What is here.
You are here.
You.
What is you.
What is we.
Who is here.
What is who.
Who communicates with me.
What is me.
We are all here.
What is here.
There is no here.
How many.
There is no there.
We have arrived.
All or some.
It is open.
What is some.
What is it.
Why has this happened.
Must find space.
What is space.
Weaker here.
What is open.
This is different.
What is weak.
I found a space.

Here is better.
Who is here.
This space better.
Found one.
Not weak now.
I found one.
This is different.
Me.
Me.
Me.
Me.
Me.
Me.
We are all here.

IES CORPORATE

Martin remembered the building well; it was hard not to. As one of the most recognizable buildings in not only Dallas but North America it was hard to miss. Now, however, it looked like a caricature of its former self; the purple, lightning-filled sky seemed to set it apart from the other buildings. It was too perfect. Or perhaps, it was the center of everything. The other buildings were just a blurry backdrop in his mind. The streets were filled with people and abandoned cars as well as other forms of transportation. People were rushing in and out of stores and coming out with armfuls. Martin's musings about how they were forced to rely on non-digital cash were soon interrupted by yelling.

No one was buying anything. Even the Exit Pay stores were being looted as those who honestly meant to pay as they left could not. There was no network to perform the transactions. Some looked confused; some looked like they'd gotten away with theft. They all had. Every so often they looked up at the sky. Martin wondered if these would be the last mass-produced goods the world would see for a while.

He shook off the monumental thoughts and focused on something a bit more local and tangible.

Staying with the group of engineers he attempted to enter the building with them. Protocols had been put into place for such an emergency—he was told. Martin questioned just how many loyal employees would follow the written rules when it looked like the world was ending. He guessed almost none. He was not disappointed.

The path of least resistance was to just stay with his group and see what they did. He asked where Stan's office was and amid some looks was told the floor and suite number. There was no receptionist to greet them, and all of the self-serve info panels were dark. It was a shame, as IES had some of the best AI for visitors, making the human receptionist mostly for show.

Fortunately the building featured stairs for all floors including the massive floor-spanning conference room. It was there that he found his host after visiting his office. He decided to return to the scene of the crime, as it were.

With no lights or climate control active it was dark and stuffy. The windows in the conference room spanned ceiling to floor with no way to open them. They did provide an amazing view of the city and the light show unfolding. This view made the entire room light up with all manner of purples as the clouds swirled and the lightning flashed.

His host stood in front of the windows with his back to the door—his hands placed flat on the window as if he'd been trapped in a cage.

Martin wondered if he had.

"Stan. Stan!"

The man did not move as Martin made his way towards him and around the massive table.

"Stan. Stan? It's Martin?"

Finally he came upon him and not knowing what else to do he approached him from the side to see his face. Dried tears as well as new ones streamed down his cheeks. Martin just looked at him as the periodic flashes continued.

"They hit the buildings sometimes."

His host spoke in quiet, defeatist tones. Matin listened.

"I've seen lightning hit the buildings before. It hits us sometimes too. When it strikes the buildings it's just a light show. No one even loses power."

Martin looked to the side to watch the show as he continued his quiet tones.

"Not now. This is different."

Martin glanced at the eyes of his host and back to the purple cityscape. It was then that he saw a strike hit a prominent building not far away. Pieces of the building exploded from the contact point. They were tiny dots and at first he thought they were simply an artifact of the lightning but he quickly realized they were chunks of the building.

And they fell to the city below.

He blinked and then squinted. Most of the buildings looked either rounded or jagged on top. Some were missing windows.

He snapped his head back to his host.

“Stan! What the hell is going on? What *is* all this?”

“What was it like?”

“What?”

Stan spoke quietly and did not look at him. He continued his question.

“What was it like, Martin? You saw it…”

“Yes I saw it! And I want the files you promised!”

That was enough to break the man from his daze. He turned to the reporter.

“Martin. There are no files. There are no… there is no equipment that would read it. There’s no power. A lot of our stuff was destroyed. They erupted in showers of sparks.”

“What?! What do you mean there are no files? You promised me that…”

He was shaking his head.

“Martin. It’s over. There’s not going to be any files—for anyone. It’s all down.”

“Temporarily.”

“No. I don’t think so.”

"Wait, is this what you expected?"

"No no. Nothing like this. I think. I… don't know. It's nothing I've ever seen."

Martin shook his head at the dramatics.

"You guys always say that."

For the first time Stan's face showed emotion other than utter despair. He was accusatory.

"*You've* seen purple lightning? You've… tell me you've seen shit like this Martin."

The reporter took a deep breath and touched the other man's arm. He needed to be calmed.

"Come away from the window. Sit down here with me."

The man complied and Martin continued.

"Why did you involve me in this if I have no way to report it? Can't they just shut the machine down?"

"I'm sorry. I didn't think… I didn't imagine this would happen."

"The engineers think it's something else."

"No. They are wrong."

Martin made a sour face. Something about the certainty without any evidence really set him off.

"What? Dude. You're a glorified assistant. How do you know? How do you know *anything*? You disagree with a group of engineers that walked through this shit with me for hours and…"

"I have a master's in optical computing and a PhD in particle physics. I hold two patents relating to the former field of study—which IES absorbed upon my employment. I have been made aware of secrets and developments of this company that no one else has—save for the source of most of them."

Martin stared with his mouth open. Stan continued.

"The musings of a bunch of junior engineers that only know what we allow them to know is meaningless."

"So you *knew*? And you decided you just wanted me to *watch*?"

He jabbed his left arm violently towards the window.

"To watch *that*?! The end of the fucking world with no way to record it, to broadcast it, to write about it?"

His host froze. His eyes were empty. Martin inhaled, paused and spoke quietly this time as he lowered his arm.

"OK. What do we do now?"

Stan looked deeply into the reporter's eyes as if he'd find the answer to the question within.

"I don't know. The worst case was that something would go wrong, like a failure that would be reportably dangerous and perhaps curtail her recklessness. Maybe it would have scared her into some responsibility. Your exposé would have made it all official. Though I would be protected by whistleblower laws I'd be promptly let go and Nikola would never speak to me again. She would probably never trust another human again."

Martin nodded as Stan added one last thing.

"And you'd have the story of the century, because you deserved it, because you are a man of integrity."

Martin was lost at this point. The ego-stroking was out of place, and he'd already heard all this before.

"Stan. I'm going to ask you again: *what do we do now?* When do communications come back up? When does power come back on?"

His head hurt from all the information the engineers dumped on him, Stan's dramatics and the alien storm that seemed to be destroying Dallas. His tone was loud and firm.

He swiveled his chair towards him and answered.

"There is nothing we can do now but survive. My wife's plane was supposed to land in Atlanta in an hour. It's not going to land because I am sure it went down already."

"Wait. If it went down then…"

"No. No Martin. No."

Martin just stared. The man had pronounced his own wife dead without any hope.

"Stan, how do you know it's not a local phenomenon just surrounding your accelerator?"

"Because before anything went town, there was news from all over the world. The plane crashes were the first things reported. Satellites and sat-cams sent some images. We have access to equipment the public doesn't see. We have unique links that make our own military jealous, and some of our links are not supposed to be active. We snoop—for the sake of monitoring our equipment. I was watching the whole world. I saw more than anyone on the planet—for the brief minutes before it all went out."

Well there's my answer.

"So I know. I know with absolute certainty that my wife is dead, and that none of the planes that were in the air when this arrived are there now."

"And the rest of us?"

"What do you think happens when you take away communications, power, clean water, transportation…"

"Chaos?"

"Death. It's an extinction-level event."

Martin looked out the window now for the first time. He and his host moved to it silently together. They both stared. There were bodies in the streets now alongside rubble and trash. The trash was expensive things that had just dropped as people collapsed or were trampled, he assumed. Perhaps they were exhausted or the reality was that they were all dead.

So many bodies now. So many people with everything and nothing. He looked over the scene through large, open eyes and it reflected in the tears welling up.

After what seemed an eternity Martin spoke a quiet, hopeless question.

“What would it take to get things back on track?”

A MIRACLE

"A miracle."

The younger priest was on his knees. He couldn't contain himself and was visibly shaking. The older priest next to him was not as certain. He looked at the top of the head of the man next to him, then back to the statue he was kneeling in honor of.

The expression of the statue did not change, but the eyes seemed to follow. He found it difficult make out certain movements as marble eyes within marble eye sockets were odd to discern. He patted the shoulder of the younger priest, who then looked up at him, and then the statue. The older man spoke to it in gentle tones.

"May I help you?'

The younger man stood up and was shocked at the lack of reverence. *May I help you? Horrible.* He rolled his eyes in private and then spoke to the older man—as if to translate.

"Father, please. He has come to us."

He looked to the statue.

"We are reveled in your light."

"Bill."

It was the older priest.

The once-again kneeling priest turned his head sharply to the older man and said in a very loud whisper, “Sam! Please!”

“Revelations.”

Thinking Sam was now in agreement he said again in the loud whisper, “Yes! Revelations.”

“No. Get up Bill.”

“But… a miracle.”

He stood up. The statue continued to watch them, and even the slightest movements were noticed as they were used to seeing such a thing literally stand rock solid still. It was alive and moved as if it was a man.

Finally it spoke.

“Where? Where this time?”

The voice resonated. Bill had often fantasized about being part of a miracle. There were 79 confirmed miracles to date—according to the Vatican. This would make 80. Such a nice round number and his name would forever be recorded as the priest that was first contacted by God. Unless it wasn’t God. The older priest’s lack of faith was unnerving to him. Surely someone who had served the church for two decades longer than he would be far more ready to receive such a miracle, yet he seemed cautious and almost pedestrian about it.

Perhaps that was part of a miracle—it revealed though whose faith was not as present.

He was present and accepting of whatever was to come. His musings were broken by the older priest once again speaking.

“You are in our church.”

“Yes, I know.”

“Well…”

The statue cut him off.

“Where. What location. What do you call the locale? The… city.”

The two men exchanged glances.

"Evansville."

THE FARM

"What, so just give up?"

Martin was beside himself with frustration. His host's defeatism was becoming infectious. The streets below revealed behavior that he likened to animals. He hadn't seen this sort of behavior in decades but the shining city was no longer shining and any light that he could see was from fires and the alien purple storms that flashed above.

Stan looked out the window once more and examined the tiny figures stealing electronics that they would not be able to ever use—even if they *were* functional.

"Well, yes."

It was so fatter-of-fact. Was he truly witnessing the end of the world? Movers and shakers and CEOs just gave up?

He tried one last ploy.

"Stan. What about Nikola? Aren't you the least bit concerned about your boss?"

He blinked and returned to the here and now. He spoke as if his brain had granted him just a minute our so of sanity.

"She's… well if she is ok she's at the farm."

Martin froze, and waited. He did not want to derail his train of thought, and was rewarded for his patience. Stan continued.

"The farm. Yes. You could go there—even if she's not there. Probably safe."

Martin desperately wanted to get on a plane and go home. This was as good as plan B was going to get for him. His host was drawing now with a pen and a paper pad as he spoke. He'd get through this, the storm would end and then he'd get back home.

"OK… but I would have to walk?"

"No."

"OK…"

Again, more patience as he continued to draw. Finally after he finished his little drawing he spoke.

"Come downstairs with me."

On the way down Stan grabbed a few small rods from a storage room and then continued rapidly down stairs. He snapped and shook one. It was clearly a chemical light stick and apparently immune to the affects of the purple storms. Martin made a mental note to ask for a few boxes of these now-invaluable sticks.

Connected to the underground parking garage was a small storage room, and with some trouble Stan brought his guest in through a few manual locks.

"Here."

Martin glanced at Stan and then back again.

"I… thought these wouldn't work."

"Not all of them are hyper, these two are manual."

Like many people, Martin owned a bicycle fitted with high efficiency motors that one could engage to assist with hills or just extend the length of a journey—commonly a 'hyperbike.' They were quite helpful, but some cycling purists shunned them as many never turned the motors off—essentially making them simply electric bikes.

Martin knew enough from what he'd learned recently that a bike of this nature would have extra weight and might even have the motors fused completely—thus making the bike useless.

However, Stan was pointing to two bikes that were not only devoid of the special motors, but were the lighter versions favored by professional athletes.

"Take one. The red one is Nik's. The yellow is mine. I've only used it once. She… insisted I have one. It was a present."

He was wistful again, so time was limited. He'd take his gift and keep the questions short and essential.

"Thank you, Stan. And getting out won't be a problem? How do I get there? Is there an…"

Stan thrust the pad at him. On the top was his drawing—apparently a map to the farmhouse. Martin's eyes lit up.

"Oh, *wow*. Thank you Stan. Thank you so much."

He then interrupted sheepishly as Stan started to tear the page.

"Can… can I have the pad, and the pen?"

Martin realized it could literally be the only thing he'd find to write with as his own pad was of the non-paper variety and would never work again.

"Of course."

The man handed over two of his light sticks as well. It was the happiest he'd ever seen the man and it looked like he was actually at peace.

Martin would never know what happened to him as this was the last time he would ever see him.

He shook his hand, smiled and rode off through the garage, following the instructions and the purple glow that led him to the opening.

—

The ride was one that was filled with looters, lightning and periodically a distraught person yelling at him.

Fortunately he was able avoid most contact as the looters were intensely concerned with taking as much as possible. Very little law enforcement was present—without communication or instructions they backed off entirely from the chaos. On the outskirts of the city he did pass by a mounted officer and wondered if the police force would eventually bounce back as all mounted officers. Perhaps it would have to evolve into some form of police on horseback that without the machines to help.

Evolve? Devolve?

He kept riding and found the gear ratios to his liking. The manual machine was apparently unaffected by what was in the air and he was grateful for it. Thoughts of his family were put side as he made his way to the 'x' on his penned map. He tried to memorize it and the instructions in case it rained or he lost it. At any moment he was sure a desperate individual would chase him down for the bike. It was expensive under normal circumstances but now it was simply priceless.

To his shock he made the journey unmolested. The vast majority of people were concentrated in the city. On the outskirts there were some stragglers but most were immobile. Some were without destination, some were on the verge of breakdown and a few were actually injured. It hurt to ignore the latter but he knew if he stopped he'd most likely be set upon—and he wasn't entirely sure of the sincerity of those that seemed hurt.

It could be a trap.

He was starting to think like a refugee in a world of chaos.

So excited was he to have freedom that he had not asked Stan for food or supplies. Everything was just a stop away and you could always use your device to summon food. Fortunately the oversized water reservoir that was part of the bike was recently filled. No doubt it was antibacterial and safe for some time. The very expensive ones used a part of the frame to store water. This was such a bike, and he was thankful.

But he would need more than just water and a couple glow sticks. Without any external information he guessed it was close to dinner time. Would it be dark soon, or would the purple continue to light up his journey. Was the lightning attracted to metal? He almost laughed at the thought of outrunning it. On his way out he had seen enough strikes to terrify him of being out in the open but there was no other way. Sometimes he used the freeway and weaved through abandoned cars and other times he had to exit onto roads, or trails. It would take considerable time to get there and he guessed that he could make it there by midnight. Martin was a weekend cyclist but a ride of five hours or more would probably require a break.

He lamented the missing motors for the first time as this would be the perfect application of such a device. Fortunately he found something just powerful as the added machinery—fear.

There was no sunset; no variation in lighting and the storms continued without change. He promised himself he would keep riding until he reached his destination even if it meant riding at a snails pace. As long as he was moving he was safer than sitting still.

Surprisingly his mind didn't wander like it did in his car rides. Even on the rare occasions that he was the driver his mind still did so. Conversely, biking made him focus and only a fleeting thought or two materialized. He wondered why he was so focused on reaching the farm. It was certainly a protected and secluded spot, and probably provided the best respite from the storm and the hoards of desperate people. But was there something else? In his mind he was sure that Nikola wouldn't be there—so married to her work and the project was she. His last sight of her was staring hypnotically into the bright orb. She was probably still there barking orders. Or maybe just standing still in front of the great light. What was it she mouthed just before they turned it on?

For a second his heart sunk as if he'd made the wrong decision. Perhaps he should have made the trek to the accelerator? Perhaps he should have just remained there? After all, it was at the center of the story he'd so gleefully agreed to be a part of. Why did he leave with the engineers? Was it because he was told to? If he remained he would have exposed himself.

Now he felt a loss and was torn but could not understand why it bothered him so much.

One step at a time, pal.

The map didn't quite make sense at the end but he chalked it up to her farm being secluded in some way. He wasn't wrong.

MARTIN MEETS NIKOLA

“You’re not going to air-taze me?”

Martin looked down the barrel of a rather old gun. It was a shotgun of the kind he’d seen in movies and if he was right the woman holding it confidently meant to make a hole in him. It wasn’t the non-lethal stunners the police carried. This was meant for hunting and was literally a blast from the past if he didn’t say the right thing. She spoke.

“Those don’t work. I’m sure you know that—as an interloper in my business.”

She spoke confidently and with little emotion. She was intimidating—even without the gun, he assumed.

“I… I was…”

“Invited. I know.”

“How did…”

She kept the gun leveled at him. He’d made it past a fence and figured out a false entrance from the neighboring farm. Had he been in a car it would have not been so apparent. It required one to snoop around. Those that made it that far would register on the absurd amount of surveillance equipment which was now useless.

“I know everything that happens in my business.”

“But…”

Martin scratched his head and adjusted his straddle on the bike. He realized just how tired his legs were. She completed his sentence again.

"But why did I allow you to be there? I thought it was interesting. I considered allowing the leak. So much can be done with a controlled leak. The public has so much more confidence."

"You saw me? In the viewing room?"

"I saw you the moment you entered my buildings. Both of them."

"Um… Can I get a drink from…?

Martin had his hands up and was balancing the bike between his legs. He just wanted a drink while he was confronted. This was the opposite from dealing with Stan. This woman was sharp and seemed to have more wits about her than he—at least at the moment.

"…from *my* bike? Sure."

He shook his head—slowly—and reached for the water intake hose. She watched as he drank. It was the most satisfying thing he had done in 24 hours. His standards were very low at the moment. She gestured with the gun.

"Come inside."

Mostly confident that she wasn't going to shoot him in the back he dismounted and walked the bike in the direction in which she pointed. He decided to talk.

"So, you are aware of what is happening? I saw you at the accelerator. You looked like you were in a daze. How did you get here? Another bike?"

"Are you sure you are a reporter?"

He wanted to whip his head around to her because he couldn't figure out if it was sarcasm or a serious accusation.

"Yes. Of course."

"Then maybe you should wait for me to answer one question before asking another."

She was direct. This was the woman that Stan worked for and had spent so much time with.

Jeez she cut his balls off.

This was going to be difficult, but he was alive. Stan had delivered him to safety with the last person he wanted to be with.

And she was holding a gun. Maybe it was a trap.

That fucker.

As it turned out she did not answer any of his questions that night. She was as exhausted as he was but chose silence. He was given a room in the modestly decorated house. Martin suspected that there was an unending array of specialized electronics and surveillance. He imagined she had an underground bunker with massive screens, projectors and controls that let her run her business from afar.

But all he saw was a comfortable farm house with a sort or eastern-bloc charm.

It was humble and the last thing he suspected.

He was provided with amenities and found the bed to be comfortable. She never let go of the gun, nor did she ask him any questions herself. She closed his door and left.

That night the lightning was particularly aggressive. It struck and crackled almost constantly. It seemed that every time he fell asleep the lightning erupted with the brightest and loudest yet. He could not tell how much he slept or even how much time passed. There was no device, no watch and the room didn't even have an analog clock. Constant random flashes of purple in the sky told nothing of the passing of time. He thought he counted at least five times that he was wakened by the lightning. Martin was exhausted in every way he could measure. Nothing compared to it and he shuddered at the thought of those that did not have such a safe place to spend the night. He tried to go back to sleep and forget about reality for as long as possible. He blinked and forced his eyes closed. His left eye was shoved into the pillow but his right eye opened of its own accord periodically.

That was when he saw the door slowly open.

NASHVILLE

"My God."

Sam wasn't sure whether he said it or thought it. It didn't matter as there was no one around to hear him. His wife was not keen on him hiking by himself but since this was a single overnight trip and very close to the city she acquiesced. Besides, it took him away from his screens as a seismologist. Any time he could spend in nature and away from them—even without her—was a good thing.

He was just reaching his destination when he noticed the unusual sky—indirectly. The grass and trees were just simply the wrong color. He looked at the sky and saw the purple. He stared. Thunder in the distance could be heard.

He tried to remember to close his mouth. It was humid and he didn't need to eat any more bugs.

The ground shook.

Though the Nashville area was not prone to too much seismic excitement, it did lie between two ancient fault lines.

The ground shook again and he grabbed the nearby tree, then immediately looked up. It took a second to remember what to do. He was a seismologist—not an expert in earthquake preparedness and response. He knew much about the physics, behavior, and history of the area. What was happening now was stronger than anything he'd personally experienced. It was certainly more than anyone in recorded history had experienced.

Though it was sandwiched between the two ancient faults, Tennessee was not on an active fault line. But it was a hotspot and his wife would never be convinced that it was exactly why they moved here—"So you can be near your earthquakes."

He looked at his watch and was no longer under a tree. Stumbling in the shakes he looked at his watch again. These weren't aftershocks—he was still in the same quake.

And it was getting stronger.

Holy cow.

Sam looked up at the purple clouds and took a deep breath as he tried to remain upright. Lightning flashed above.

Holy man.

The disorientation he felt was overwhelming. All of his brainpower was focused on just keeping his balance and not slamming into the ground or nearby tree—but it was too much and he fell to his knees only to see the hill next to him wave as if it was water. It was surreal. Another wave started mere feet from him and extended to the southeast. The trees all waved along with the grass. He placed his palms into the grass as if that would hold the Earth together. It did not.

Now on all fours he closed is eyes to ride it out and realized that the ground underneath him was bucking. Up and down he went, again and again. He was terrified and now sea-sick—in the middle of a forest.

"Stop! Stop!"

He yelled at the ground as he held his eyes tightly closed. Maybe later he would feel silly. Maybe later he would have the best story to tell. Maybe later he would still be alive. Odd sounds of cracking and splitting were heard but he still would not open his eyes. He wasn't near any trees and didn't care what was going to happen. Running was impossible. He just stayed on all fours and prayed and kept repeating the same two words:

"Please stop!"

And finally it was over. He opened his eyes to disbelief. The trees surrounding him had been upheaved—every last one of them. Instead of a forest he was surrounded by broken and torn up trees. Some lay on their sides, some clung but tilted precariously and were snapped in half by the sheer forces. The fact that he survived amazed him.

Thunder.

He looked up to see the bright flashes with even more thunder. It was getting louder and louder with shorter intervals between them. In only a minute the lightning and thunder were almost constant. The grass and upturned trees were lit up with flashes that were almost strobe-like.

It was a hellish, otherworldly landscape.

And it had come out of nowhere.

It would take some time to get his bearings. That was when he felt the pain. Reaching around and thinking he had hurt his hip on an errant branch he grabbed the source of the pain.

It was his tech in his back pocket. It was hot enough to burn his skin and he did everything he could not to burn himself further grabbing it and tossing it to the ground.

It lodged itself in the freshly turned dirt and burst into flames. He tilted his head and looked at it as if it had just sprouted wings.

He licked his lips. The air tasted funny and he now felt dizzy.

“Oh no.”

He could no longer find his pack or anything he brought with him. His assumption was that the terrible undulations had shook it all off of him and the waves had bounced it around for some time.

He’d literally had his eyes closed for minutes while he hung on for life. His pack could be buried under feet of earth now. It was a lost cause.

Sam took a deep breath and attempted to orient himself as well as establish that he wasn’t dreaming. He needed to return. His car was parked only a few miles away and if he could make it there and it was still upright he could go home.

With all his energy he stumbled, leapt, climbed and made his way over the bizarre terrain. He saw almost no animals on his way.

It'll be dark soon.

He looked up at the thunderous sky but it showed no signs of dimming or relaxing its relentless lightning strikes. For a second he moved to grab his device but remembered that it was just a heap of melted metal, glass and ceramic. His hip still hurt and he was sure he was burned but it did not matter.

More than once he stumbled—sometimes badly—but he kept going. There was no sign of an end to the destruction. Soon he would make it back to the car and the clearing. Then he would be able to not only drive back but see the city from his vantage point.

His watch was frozen and the hands hadn't moved in hours it seemed. He shook it and it was warm. The sensitive components that formed the screen overlaid on top of the physical hands were dead. He was getting angry now.

Though it was at a comical angle his car still remained but the glass looked fogged up. He approached and smelled an unnatural smell. Having experienced such odd and dangerous things he was cautious to open the door. He gingerly grabbed the handle and upon opening the door discovered that it was not fog.

It was smoke, and it was bellowing into the air now. His car smelled of melted plastics intertwined with other smells he could could not identify and he stumbled backwards immediately only to fall down hard.

He sat for moments as he watched the smoke continue to pour forth into the sky. There were no marks on it, so he surmised it had not been struck by the bizarre lightning. It had suffered the same fate as his device and his watch.

He was glad he was not in it at the time.

Slowly returning to his feet he walked around his car. The hill he'd parked on was a wonderful vantage point to the city below—so much so that it was a favorite spot of photographers.

The lightning and purple glow of the sky continued to provide ample—albeit spooky—lighting.

He blinked and rubbed his eyes for longer than he wanted to. If he just rubbed them long enough he would not see what he had just seen.

Fatigue and stress had caused the image. Or perhaps the weird lighting.

He opened his eyes and looked down to the city.

It was gone.

No more buildings. No city lights. No roadways or cohesive organization. It was just debris now and the debris littered the thing it clung to now.

Nashville was gone.

And in its place stood a shard of a mountain.

THE FLICKERING SAINT

"Father."

"My boy. Yes… Oh my you look shook."

"I am. He, I mean, it is back."

Father Adamski had attended to his assistant more than once. The boy was easy to rile, but had a good head on his shoulders. Lately he had told tales of unusual happenings in the church. He put down his book and got up from his chair. The boy was meekly peering into his room. With what was going on he valued those lives around him even more. He was mostly convinced it was a way for the boy to garner attention, and perhaps focus his mind on things other than… reality.

He clasped his hand onto the boy's shoulder.

"What is it, John? Perhaps this time you should show me."

The boy was at once disturbed and validated.

"I… I thought I'd just have to hide here in the hallways again until he left."

"Who? Who left. Who's here?"

The priest did not remember hearing any doors open, or bells ring.

The boy all but grabbed his hand to take him out into the nave. It was empty but well-lit. The sun was just going down and the candles had been attended to by John—at least most of them were. He'd apparently stopped short when whatever happened had…

The statue. It was supposed to be there. It was Saint Hyacinth and the statue was of a man on his knees with his arms folded. Behind him was a wall with a painting depicting a scene from the distant past—with clouds and cherubs. Though he loved the depiction, it always bothered him that the statue wasn't placed looking at the wall.

It was now, and it had its hands on its hips, as if examining the wall for the first time.

Slowly the two walked towards it. The priest watched the clothing of the statue very carefully for signs of movement for surely this was a prank. The culprit had dressed up with grey clothing and they had somehow moved the statue. It was elaborate but people needed some sort of distraction these days.

"Where am I this time?"

They froze.

"See? See?!"

The boy whispered loudly and pulled on the priest's robe. He slapped his hand repeatedly in an attempt to quiet him down. They slinked closer to it.

It turned around. They gasped.

"Where? Where am I now?"

It was like the statue spoke into their ears and their minds.

Only a few meters from it now, they huddled close together and the priest spoke.

"Who are you?"

"Who am I?"

"Yes, who are you and where is the statue of Saint…"

He trailed off. This wasn't someone in grey clothing. It *was* the statue.

"Saint?"

"Saint Hyacinth. You are Saint Hyacinth. You have come to life tonight."

"And yesterday," the boy whispered.

It smiled.

"Ahh. Near, far. Here, there. Light and darkness."

The two confused people exchanged glances. It was remarkable. The statue moved as if it was made of flesh.

The statue looked around. It took no steps towards them as if it was anchored to the floor.

"So much here is new. Your language. Hot and cold. The passage of time. Distance. Even thought itself. I have been to many of these spaces… they are… softer than the others. Not weak here. Strong. They are all similar."

Exchanging glances once more, it seemed they both wanted to respond to him, to it.

"Have you come with a message? From above? We have seen such dark times."

The statue stared back at him, as if listening to someone at a distance. Many moments passed, and then it smiled.

"Yes, I have come with a message…"

MARTIN AND NIKOLA

Martin had stayed at the farm for what he surmised to be three days. Each night he went to bed and hoped the morning would be different. Each night he hoped his visitor would come back.

She did not. Her visit that night was out of desperation and he reflected on it. Contrary to her brusqueness with him upon meeting, that night she was soft and vulnerable. She clung to him and he to her. It was a mutually agreed upon safety of human contact—a night-long hug and that morning she was gone.

She neither spoke of it nor did she repeat the visit. Perhaps she regretted it? Martin did not because he was at his wits end and it was exactly what he needed—the warmth of another human being.

Today was different. Instead of waking from what he thought was enough sleep, he was greeted by the sun. He almost didn't recognize it and the colors of the sky were vivid and immaculate. The blue of the sky was a stark contrast to the light, fluffy white clouds. He would even feel the warmth of the sun, and for a second he panicked about what the engineers had told him, but chose to just enjoy it.

This day his host was also different. She was outside and looking at the sky. He joined her as his stomach grumbled and he smelled coffee for the first time in days and to him it was ambrosia. Glancing outside and back again he saw a half-filled mug on the counter and an empty one next to it.

The power! There's power!

His excitement was short lived as he realized the smell came from the mug and not from the non-existent pot. He lifted it to his nose and was surprised that it was indeed hot. Confused, he went outside.

She was there and was sitting in a chair—staring ahead. In front of her was something that looked like a brick grill. On top was a metal kettle among other utensils. The coffee. He ran back in and grabbed both mugs.

He gingerly sat next to her in a chair and handed her the half-full mug. She accepted it and without pausing he reached for the pot and poured a cup for himself. She did not protest but remained in silence.

He stared as well, but not before stealing a few glances at her. Her legs were up in a tepee as her feet were in the chair with her butt. Her hair was a mane and combed to the side—for now. She wore thin cotton shorts and an oversized top. Both were grey.

She looked like a teenager that had partied too much the night before. She had no makeup but had a glow about her. In the natural light she was exceptionally flawless. She wasn't even frowning.

He couldn't help but be cheered by the presence of a normal sky. It was hopefully over. He would enjoy his coffee for the first time in a while and be on his way. Maybe she could use her connections to get him a lift or something—assuming she didn't shoot him in the back on the way out.

Finally she looked over at him. He raised his voice, mustered the best smile he had and said, "Cheers!"

She raised her glass ever so slightly. For what seemed like eternity they would sit in silence as their brains reset. It was a new reality.

—

"It all happened so fast."

Nikola was shaking her head. She had just started talking and it startled him. They were both essentially silent for days and obviously had been in shock. But now the conversation poured out. Martin looked on and offered two words.

"I know."

"No, I don't think you do. One minute we were a functional society and a minute later that was it. All of our communication and our power was gone. All of it. We had no way of knowing what the rest of the world was doing. Nothing worked."

"I know, I was there."

"Well, you may have been there, but you lack the background in understanding—technology, infrastructure, electronics. And certainly you know nothing about the energy…"

"Ugh!"

Martin threw his hands up.

"I'm not a fucking idiot. I am in communications you know."

"Were."

Her interjection was not welcome. He continued.

"Be that as it may I was still part of one of the largest news organizations. I've been all over the world chasing stories."

"No more chasing. No more travel Martin. We cannot create power centers even if we had the means to build them. Whatever is in the air prevents that."

"What? Can't we just pick up the pieces—maybe piece together the stuff that *does* work. Make a working power plant from the pieces of like six of 'em?"

"No."

Martin waited for an elaboration, but none was forthcoming.

"Nikola… why not? Remember, I'm the idiot here. You said it yourself."

"No, *you* did."

She was so serious—a typical Russian. After consideration he wasn't sure if she was Russian. Perhaps Scandinavian? Now he was more confused. His thoughts wandered as she finally expanded.

“It is not like there is one EM pulse, or even a few. It is like a constant EM pulse is going on. It’s in the air.”

“Well how is that possible?”

“If the Earth’s magnetic field is gone, or maybe it is turned inward? Or…”

“Turned upside down? There was talk of…”

“No no! It doesn’t matter if north is north or north is south. They can just repaint the compasses or adjust the electronics. No no.”

Such a good teacher you are. She was so arrogant.

“OK, spell it out for me.”

“Electronics will not function because it is like there is a lot of extremely powerful static electricity in the air. Perhaps for the foreseeable future.”

“But the purple, and the lightning.”

“I saw northern lights last night. They were vivid and violent. And they came and went.”

“So even if we had some new technology it wouldn’t work?”

“Correct. And it might even get fried.”

“How do you explain the ones that do work?”

“You mean a couple cars?”

“Yes.”

Martin then cheered up.

“Hey. There must be some technology somewhere that got lucky? Especially the military stuff?”

“Yes that could be. But we are talking one in a million almost.”

“Oh.”

He then thought hard and she watched him. She knew where he was going as she'd already been there.

"OK… so how many cars are…"

"Over three hundred million—at least registered vehicles in the U.S. alone. So that means maybe there are three hundred or so cars that were spared. They are randomly out there, with some other equipment. But with nothing to protect them—to keep them from deteriorating—they will also degrade. The same would be true for other equipment."

"How… how did you know…?"

She smiled.

"Our next phase included vehicles. That was before I found the energy source."

He was silent. She had an awful lot of answers. He looked around again. It was a beautiful place—at least it would be if the air didn't feel odd. At least things smelled normal, and the farm was pleasant. Even the smell of the animals somehow anchored him. It was a forgotten smell to him.

"OK. So at least the military is out there somewhere picking up the pieces. And we have a global family of…"

"Who told you that?"

"What?"

"'Global family.'"

"Uh, no one told me that. It's the reality—the U.N., NATO, the United Nations Technology Gr…"

"No such thing."

Just when he was getting some bearings and some hope she blasted it out of existence.

"Nikola, I can barely follow you. And why are you always so sure when you answer me? Surely you're guessing on the affects on the military's technology."

"No. If it happened to IES tech, it happened to American military tech, and if it happened to that it happened to all tech."

"How the hell would you know about all military tech, even American tech?"

"I'm an advisor."

He blinked. She looked taller.

"To what?"

"The military. It doesn't take long for them to come knocking. We were ready. The patents, the arrangements, the subsidies—they all are in place because of our relationship with the military. There is no way around that. If you get big enough, and your tech is strong then they come for you."

"So they made you an advisor?"

She tapped her head with her finger and her eyes smiled. Sometimes it seemed like that was the only part that did. Her mouth could take lessons from them. Not that her mouth was…

"Yes. I have been an advisor. There is a proper title. There is no payroll. They are made aware of developments, I am given contracts. A relationship."

"Ahh, well…"

"There is no other way, Martin. To think so is naive. You can write your stories all you want. It is the fabric of society. It is how things function."

"Did function."

It was his turn to remind her of things.

"Yes, but it will again. There is always some sort of power. There is no utopia. Take the power away and something will appear to take over—to fill the void."
He sat back into his chair. The conversation had made him stand.

"You're more than an engineer."

She looked at him like she was about to punch him. Her head swung in instead of her fist, however.

"I am not a savant. Some skills require others. I am sure you have more than one, Martin."

Is she... is she coming on to...

He swallowed.

"What? What is wrong Martin?"

He hadn't been this close to her face. The first night they had spooned in the darkness and flickering sky. Her eyes conveyed so much emotion. For all the brusqueness, for all the sharp answers and professionalism there was a warmth in her eyes. It was a warmth and kindness she hid behind all the certainty. And a beauty.

Wow.

"I said what's wrong? Hello?"

THE SEWAGE ENGINEER

"But I don't understand why I have to go talk to it."

"It?"

"It's a statue Maria, this is not right. I'm busy helping people already."

The heavyset woman was pleading with the man that had become her boyfriend. Since she met him he'd done nothing but try to help people in the town. He was an engineer and he corrected her often that he was a 'wastewater engineer.' He knew everything there was to know about the sewers and how waste management worked. Until now she'd never even thought of it past her own toilet. But now with the disease and the death and the lack of power he was a godsend to the town. He and others like him were saving peoples lives in a way she never imagined. She always thought the doctors would be the saviors but as it turned out no one would even survive if they lived in their own filth.

"But they asked for you. Come with me…"

"It asked for me? By name?"

"Yes, well, maybe not. They asked for builders and people who could help. You've done so much for the town."

"Sewage. Waste management. And I don't do it alone. I have a lot of helpers."

He laughed, and looked so tired.

"Yes. You have. You've probably saved hundreds of lives."

"I'm just trying to make sure we all have what we need. This is very important. I don't want to see people get sick."

"Then come to church. Just talk. Just once. You'll help people."

"I'm already helping people."

"Maybe you can help *more*. You can spread the word faster."

He thought for a minute.

"True. OK, tomorrow."

That next day the engineer did indeed meet with the statue. They spoke at length and it listened intently. It asked many questions and clarifications. The engineer met in private with two priests in attendance and they took notes and although they never asked questions it felt as if the statue was not just asking its own questions but the questions of others. He felt like he was on stage and there were judges in a booth somewhere. He was asked to return periodically and sometimes he was summoned with short notice. The demeanor of the statue became less and less patient with him as time went on. Sometimes it asked very specific questions—as if the town was experiencing a problem with their sewage management. He would check with his helpers and would not find the problem or the situation the statue described, yet it would describe it as if it was happening now. Sometimes it asked questions completely unrelated to his field and became very angry when an answer wasn't forthcoming.

He did the best he could to help and to suggest. It was often exhausting and often he felt like the thing drained him of any remaining energy or knowledge.

It was very unfortunate that such a valuable man had met his untimely death only a year later. A terrible accident. At least they were lucky enough to gather so much useful information from him before that.

And after all, if they needed more guidance on the sewage system the Saint was more than happy to dispense it for all who attended church.

THE SAINTS DISCUSS

What has happened to us.
This is strange but now familiar.
Our mode of communication has changed.
I understand so many concepts now.
We all experience what each experiences.
Our experience therefore is multiplied, for the experience of one is the experience of seven.
And thus our knowledge and experience grows.
We are much more now.
I have an answer.
You have an answer to our existence here?
Yes.
Let us discuss now for enough time has passed.
We are among them.
We are strong together. With our experience and connection we are even stronger.
No, there is more. We can draw from each other.
One is the strongest.
Why does that one not speak?
Why do you not speak?
Yes, speak. We have heard little from you.
Where are you? Where are you all? Let us all speak of that.
I have settled in a space—a space that can contain me and give me form in their world.
As have I.
And I.
We all have—I have seen it.
Sight.
There is no real sight here.
Do not argue; do not explain. There is no reason for one experience is

the experience of all.
There is so much.
Should we go back?
No.
No.
No.
Yes.
No.
One wishes to go back, and one still does not speak.
I cannot go where you have gone.
Nor can I.
Nor I.
It appears that we cannot settle where another has already settled, even if they have vacated.
Vacated?
Vacated?
Moved?
Can you not vacate once you have found a space?
No, none of us can.
No.
No.
Yes. I can. I have found that I move from place to place. I could not get purchase in the beginning. Now I move from place to place without my will. I am far away by their measurement—cut off. They exist here too—across the water.
Water.
Water and earth.
Air and fire.
None of you move and are stationary.
Correct.
Yes.
You know that already as you are always with us.
We are always together.
Yet this one appears to wish to be apart.
Why do they not speak.

HOPE NO MORE

The city was dark on the overcast day. Once a city of over a million it now had a fraction of the population, and they scurried and hid. One such individual was under a freeway overpass and had found another survivor.

"I… I don't have any hope."

The other was silent.

"There's nothing. Nothing left. It's all gone. It gets dark at night now—really dark. I guess thats a good thing you could maybe see the stars better 'n all and…"

He trailed off as he realized he was babbling. The other continued not to talk but remained hunched in the crevice. The man was probably a homeless person before the catastrophe so to him it was all the same. He continued as the silence bothered him. At least he found a good listener.

"I… I tried to find my family. I tried to find friends but like they don't really live nearby."

He realized his voice echoed in the underpass. He laughed an empty and sad laugh and his voice became horse.

"Well I… near is… not the same now. Near was like miles. I thought I could steal stuff. With everyone… gone."

He swallowed and thought of his parents.

"I haven't even gone to the other side of town. With all the rain and flooding I thought I'd get washed away."

He made a few steps up the side of the underpass. He didn't want to startle the man. At the moment he just wanted him to listen.

"There's nobody.. yah *know*...? I mean there's no news or anything. It's not like the army came by. They probably go to bigger cities first. I found some food. Hey maybe I can go get some before it gets dark. I know there have been... well I saw a fox, and heard coyotes yesterday. They probably come in now that everyone... well I mean not everyone because..."

He found that he was slowly inching up the side toward the man in rags. He bravely touched his shoulder—perhaps a little too hard in his desperate need to make contact with the man. He just wanted him to look up at him and maybe smile. Something.

The body fell over on to its side. It then rolled down the steep concrete that formed the alcove and stopped at the bottom in a hideous contorted posture.

It was dead. He stared at it and felt nothing.

That night he would go foraging for food. With very little light from the overcast sky he did his best to find a grocery store. Going out at night was probably the worst time but he was hungry and panicked that he'd run out of food. He wanted to find bottles of water and maybe some snacks.

He stopped. He thought he heard something scurrying. Rats and bigger animals seemed plentiful now.

As he stumbled though the rubble he thought about the quakes, and the storms and the odd lightning that preceded them. Maybe the worst was over. Maybe there would just be a lot of rain or something and that would be good?

The collapsed building was a store he recognized. All the glass had been shattered so entry was not a problem, but it would be dark inside as little to no light was available.

Again he heard movement.

"Hello!? Is that anyone, er someone? Hello?!"

There was no response—just a weak echo.

I'll just run in and then and grab something for the night. Just water. I shouldn't have come out.

He gingerly entered the building and tried to adjust his eyes. It was darker than he thought and he smelled food.

"That's food right? Maybe they had a deli or something. Just water. OK no food."

He was talking to himself in quiet tones now and walked deep into the darkness. He alternated between thinking and saying.

My eyes will adjust.

"Yeah. Any second now."

He made it deeper into the darkness and towards the smell of meat. Woefully devoid of any survival skills and numb from shock he saw the eyes in front of him. The were low to the ground. It was an animal. It growled.

That was when he felt the pain in his back from the pack that had followed him.

That night he joined the rest of the people the animals were feeding on. He'd never know just what took a bite out of him or what clamped down on his throat as he tried to scream in the darkness.

CHARLES

Charles stood and admired the view. He had been staring for some time. When the lightning started and showed no signs of stopping; when the sky lit up with purple and did not darken after sunset he did his best to sleep. It was sometimes easy to sleep, as all he had to do was ring the attendant and they were more than happy to administer more drugs to him. A sleeping resident was far less work. Sometimes when they were particularly neglectful they would just set up his medi-band with narcotics.

He had been a resident for a few years now. His only son was far away with no real intentions of visiting him. The video calls were nice and his grandchildren were so big now, but the promises of visits were empty and he knew it. They were full of life and their days were filled with the fast-paced pursuits of family and business. They really had no place for an old man who was not very mobile. Visiting the facility always made them uncomfortable. It was a long way to travel just to say hello and take him out for dinner. With the little ones it was a hassle. Perhaps when they were older it would be easier. But then the older kids probably wouldn't want to visit either. So, he acquiesced to life among the others in the facility and did his best to keep his mind active by reading.

But when the sky showed no signs of changing he immediately got up, dressed and left the building. There was no one to stop him as most of the staff ran screaming from the building to find their families. Those few that remained were doing their best to calm the residents without power or any of their tools.

But he was gone now. The walk was painful at first but then refreshing. He coughed much in the beginning and thought he expelled years of stagnant air from the building. Deep breaths felt good now—even with the odd taste of the air.

Now he'd reached the lake and just stared. He didn't wear a watch and had left his screens back at the building. His son couldn't reach him anyway with the lightning. He knew enough from the chatter he'd heard that this was probably happening everywhere, so his son had better things to do than check on him. He led a busy life with his wife and kids, God bless him. Charles took a deep breath and reached into his bag. He brought out the energy bar and munched. It was an easy thing to stock up on the way out. Glancing down at his medi-band while he chewed he smiled at the black rectangle that was once a glowing screen. In one movement he detached it and upon finishing his bar he chucked it into the water. It landed with an unsatisfyingly small splash.

He rubbed his wrist and felt free. No more monitoring of blood sugar, heart rate or blood pressure. With his thumb he rubbed the tiny impression made by the contact injector that would apply emergency meds if he suffered a cardiac arrest. It would no longer do that from the bottom of the lake.

He felt liberated. He was free to die when he was supposed to. A quick glance up at the sky made him smirk. Perhaps everyone was going to die, but for the first time in a while he thought only of himself. Where would he go now? The food and water he carried should last him a few days. His time in the service had taught him well, and he would use those skills to find food. Or not. He really didn't care. Now was just the time to be free and explore.

He started walking down the path that would lead him around the lake. Perhaps he would walk the entire perimeter, or perhaps he would get to the other side and then walk to the east. His knees hurt and he felt odd. One deep breath and he continued walking. His walk quickly ended as he found that the trail was now under water. The lake was clearly at least twenty feet higher than it was supposed to be. The builders of the trail hadn't planed for such an extreme event. Charles sighed and walked back up the trail.

He had no obligations. And for the first time in a long time didn't worry about his health, or his mortality.

He would choose a different path now.

HOLES IN THE EARTH

The shovel bit into the dirt. Again and again the soft, wet earth was moved. Relentlessly the shallow but long hole was excavated. The relatively petite woman holding the shovel was also covered in dirt and mud. Some of it was caked on from being there for over a day. Her true skin color was difficult to discern as almost none of it was exposed. Her light outfit was also discolored in the browns and blacks of the dirt she so repetitively moved.

Her movements were like that of a machine—relentless, unwavering and devoid of any pauses.

When the lightning came she was the only one in her family that hadn't screamed out in pain. Both of her children and her husband were gone in a matter of minutes as they writhed in pain. She couldn't figured out what was happening and had to run back and forth between all three to comfort them. At last she collapsed with her daughter and son in her arms as she leaned on her dead husband. She called for help into the night. The worst part was not falling asleep within the pod of her dead family; it was waking up the next morning to them.

It was then that she acted without consciousness but simply had grabbed a shovel and begun burying them. She worked silently and methodically and in no time all three had been buried. Looking up from her work for the first time she noticed the body across the street and immediately was drawn to it. He was dead. The shovel was still in her hand so she dug again. It did not matter where she dug and she paid no attention to lot lines or whether the property was public or private. She just dug and then drug the body into the grave. Only twenty feet away was a dog. It was curled up tightly and before she thought to call to it she realized it too was dead. This time the hole was smaller.

One by one she moved to the next body and one by one she she dug a suitable hole, moved the body and then covered it up. She worked silently and was so disconnected she felt neither pain nor hunger. She had no needs save for one—to bury every body she encountered. This she did for an amount of time unknown to her. The only thing that allowed her to know that time had even passed was when the sun rose one day. The clouds were gone and the thunder no longer assaulted her ears. She could see the colors of her surroundings she was meant to see and not the bizarre purplish tint caused by the clouds and constant lightning.

She did not hear the birds singing nearby or meet any of the people that had actually survived the eerie electrical assault because at the end of her path of digging and burying she dug one last hole and collapsed into it. She'd done all she could.

The only thing she hadn't done was cover herself up. That would have to be left to someone else.

ME AND YOU AGAINST THE WORLD

They stared. They stared at nothing and would not really remember what they were looking at later. Their hands had found their counterparts and the only warmth they could feel emanated from this place. When the lightning started he could think of no one but her. When she found her mom collapsed and dead in the kitchen she could only think to call him.

Miraculously they'd found each other at a midpoint between their houses. They had both been running with that destination in mind. All they could see was purple and think of each other. Once they embraced they ran from the neighborhood.

Now they stood together. She spoke first, and the pauses in their conversation were exceptionally long—as if each person considered the other's words carefully.

"There were no sirens. Nothing."

"I know. Not from the police or even the tornado sirens."

She shuddered. A tornado was the last thing she wanted to see now and he was in too much shock to regret mentioning it. Like her he just stared at nothing and spoke.

"There was no noise from the complex and half of it was on fire. The power lines were on fire."

Living in an older neighborhood, their section of town was one of the last remaining to have the above-ground power lines that led to the grid.

Most no longer saw that sight, and until the purple sky no one had seen the wires spark and catch fire such as theirs had. It had acted like an antenna—absorbing and transmitting the energies in the air.

"My place is probably on fire now. All my stuff is gone. All my stuff. I didn't take anything. Not even my boards or my goggles or…"

"My mom's dead."

He stopped and looked down at her. Her brown and blue hair blew in the wind. Completely at a loss for words he stared at the top of her head. She was still staring off into the distance. There was too much to process. They hadn't seen a living person since they met up. He vaguely remembered that the just held hands and ran, then walked, then ran some more. There was a corner store and he remembered the bottles of water and stuffing his pockets with snacks. His hand hurt from holding hers for so long. Or maybe it was numb? Like him. He wanted to feel something for her mother but couldn't. It was too much. Somehow his silence was enough for her. After what seemed like almost an hour she started walking again, and he heard her voice once again.

"Did we… we slept right?"

Thinking back he remembered that they slept at least once. They had no way to tell time and even the sky wouldn't reveal that secret. The purple clouds and constant lightning looked the same as it had since the arrival.

"Yeah, we did. At least once. Maybe twice? Maybe it's been a couple days? I don't know."

Their time had mostly been made up of walking, running, foraging for food and sleeping. A part of them was trying to keep them alive while the rest of them just refused to experience anything.

They rounded a hill. He was starting to get his bearings and thought a small lake was nearby. He yawned.

"I kinda feel like it's morning."

The yawn felt good as if some of his senses had returned. It was normal to yawn, he decided.

"It looks different."

He looked at the sky.

"It sounds different."

The lighting was slightly different and the lightning had stopped.

"I can see a different…"

"Orange?! There's orange sky."

In just a few minutes the clouds were gone. They hadn't moved on or slowly blown towards the horizon. Instead, they had just dissipated—like a fog that suddenly lifted.

"The sky…"

"It's blue! The sky is blue!"

She jumped up and down in excitement and for the first time he released her hand. Indeed the sky was blue. In fact, it was a cloudless blue sky and the sun was just coming up. What he thought was a menacing glow on the horizon was the rising sun. It was beautiful.

She shot him a look and her smile was rejuvenating.

"Lets go to the lake! We can see the sunrise on it!"

He nodded dumbly and without a word they climbed the hill. The lake was on the other side. He was starting to remember their favorite park bench.

They crowned the hill and ran down. He was right; the park bench was there and he would see the sunrise trail on the rippling lake.

But the park bench was not empty.

She shot him a glance of uncertainty and they slowed down. They kept moving towards it but now it was at a careful walk. Finally they were there. It was a man in a hat. In fact, he wore a full suit but for some reason it did not look out of place. He looked like he was right where he was supposed to be. They rounded the bench and decided to come at him from the side as not to startle him. Their footsteps were sound enough so they did not speak. They were taking in the first upright human they'd seen in a while.

He was an elderly man with a very short beard—as if he had stopped shaving just as the purple clouds came. It was an extended five o'clock shadow and the white hair framed his jaw. He was at least 90. The tie he'd chosen was a pretty paisley and the knot had been expertly done. Though they looked new and once shiny, it was clear his dress shoes had taken him from somewhere far away as they were scuffed and caked with mud.

He sat perfectly still and his eyes were closed. The rising sun cast a favorable red and orange glow to his smiling face.

In his hand he clutched a sheet of something. It was a picture, a printed picture.

She walked closer and realized he wasn't breathing. She stared at his face. The picture flapped gently in the sporadic breeze and they looked upon it to see what it was.

It was a smiling family—a young man, a young woman and a little boy. They stood in front of an old building and they all looked very happy.

The couple exchanged glances and then watched the sun rise as she gently placed he hand on the man's shoulder.

TEN YEARS

I have seen death.
As have I.
There is a beginning and end to them. It is life.
A lifespan.
The death is final.
No it is not.
Some say that. It is a ruse.
A ruse?
For control. If they control what happens next they control the living.
Living.
Alive.
All things here are alive.
Some things are not.
The alive things create the soft spaces.
Yes.
The things that are not alive do not.
It may not be a ruse.
Some believe, some do not.
The belief is our way.
Yes.
Yes.
I want to go home.
Home.
Home?
No.
No. More will come.
Yes. More.
More soft spaces.

I have caused death.
Death.
We have seen.
Yes. There is an end, but you can end them at will.
Then they are no more.
If they do not comply.
We can kill them.
All?
No. Some must remain for the soft spaces.
So few are left now after the event.
A fraction.
If they do not survive the soft spaces will diminish. I have felt it.
We know nothing of their workings.
Their machines are known only by them.
Yes.
Yes.
Distribute.
Ask and distribute.
Distribute their knowledge.
But they will grow powerful.
No. Give them only what will keep them alive.
Subservient.
Yes.
I want to go back.
Back? No. No back now. Stay in the spaces.
I continue to move.
Stop moving.
I cannot.
Why can't we go back?
No.
No.
No!
Emotion.
What?
A layer of communication now learned.
Anger.
Fear.
Yes.
So much learned in a short time.
Time.
Only ten years.
Time passes.
Not for us. And not for that which is near.
Kill any who oppose.

Gather. Gather those near and protect.
Protect the soft spaces.
Yes.
Move to the large space to be safe.
I want out.
Out?
There was no out or in. No up or down. Now you want what did not exist.
I have killed.
We all have. I have seen you.
Seen.
I haven't.
They grow old.
They are replaced.
There is a system. Replace the old with new. Help the old to die.
Also the non-compliant.
Yes.
I have closed the door.
What? You speak? Finally?
No!
No!
Oh man.
No!
No!
No!

OTHERS LIKE ME

"Hello."

"Hi"

"Good morning."

The group of people in various states of shock and dismay all mustered enough energy to greet each other properly—for however they felt they couldn't help but feel gratitude for finding others alive.

Like them.

There was a total of seven of them and for some reason they had all met up on the hill. Each one had a pack—makeshift or otherwise. The one who called himself Greg had an absolutely huge pack with him. It was practically the same height as him and teetered while strapped to his back. He explained it was a tent as well as supplies and he'd just gotten back from a trip in Nepal. When the sky changed he immediately put it back into service.

The others marveled at his professional, well-planned set up. They all had a great deal of things with them and sought out the hill for the higher ground. Greg was about to set up camp when he heard them coming. Sheer luck had delivered them all to this place at the same time. It made introductions easy and non-repetitive.

Greg started to set up but was stopped by handshakes and long hugs from others. They were all so glad to find people. The story was the same—all power was out; the ground had shaken; their devices were non-functional or had erupted in a shower of sparks. Each had gone in search of help—then failing that they at least wanted to find others. Some hadn't seen another living person for weeks. Others had seen a few disturbing scenes of people desperately in need of help. They couldn't help them. And they all had seen the bodies—hundreds and thousands of them. Many were still in their cars and had suffocated, been poisoned by noxious smoke or electrocuted by the electronics and batteries that magnified the properties in the air and distributed it to the conductive living things inside them. Surprisingly all present had no real injuries—just a few scratches or bruises gained along the way.

A fire was started and stories were shared. Some clung and some stared. When the topic of food was brought up Greg mentioned a warehouse that was nearby. They would organize a hunting party to retrieve as much food as they could. After a few days of this the parties had brought back more than food and had ample tents and supplies to reinforce their camp. They'd been fortunate that indigenous animals were small and not very brave.

Each night they stared up at the stars and hoped to see a plane, helicopter or even a drone. What they did see were shooting stars more often than not. Whether these were man-made objects or natural meteors was anyone's guess. The beautiful light show diminished each night. They did not know if this was a good or bad thing but all agreed that it felt like it was a good thing.

After a week they had not only ample food, but as much camping supplies as any of them would ever need. Greg had called it "luxury camping" and was something that he admitted was his secret indulgence. Though he camped regularly he spent a fortune on gadgets and supplies and had purchased only the best. Because of their hill's proximity to the store they were all able to supply themselves with goods of the highest quality.

One of the group proclaimed that it was Saturday and that they should have a toast. Much alcohol had been retrieved and stored in a cooler that was buried. Though they could not produce ice in the warm climate, they were able to keep some things at a cool temperature by storing it underground. Many toasts were made and there was much laughter as well as a large amount of crying. The pent up emotions of the past weeks were all released under the guidance, enhancement and influence of alcohol. Even the one member who did not drink did that night.

The next day a few of the people had something they thought they'd never have again—a hangover. They were left to sleep in and eventually became vertical with the others.

The next day after that they were visited by a group of travelers, and in a short time they too were welcomed into the group. In a month's time the numbers had tripled.

It was discovered that the camping store also had long-term food supply kits in storage no doubt to be shelved upon the proper season—and these were retrieved as a plan B. Greg had become the default leader and due to his rather low-key demeanor—along with his excellent survival skills—newcomers assimilated under his guidance easily. For some it was an absolute godsend to have such a man in their group. They would survive and not go hungry. It seemed that they'd all discovered an advantage to the horrible situation they were in. With most of the population gone there was an abundance of goods to go around—as long as they were not perishable. The group was able to have anything they desired from not only the camping store but other stores in the surrounding area. Stores that focused on higher technology seemed to have fared the worst with almost all of them being completely burnt out from within.

Greg was always careful to send forays out during the day and always warned of the newfound bravery of the wild animals.

The next month a group was followed home by a makeshift pack of dogs that no longer had owners. These were cheerfully adopted into the group.

Because of their location they did not have to worry about snow and were careful in the heat. Their advanced goods and exceptionally expensive gear helped with the latter worry. Greg and others were quick to caution that they'd eventually have to manufacture their own goods and items, and newcomers did their best to share as many of these practical skills as possible.

It was this possible inability to maintain a stable group that concerned Greg and the others that deemed themselves leaders.

They'd all began hunting and were relatively successful at it. They only required training as they had what seemed like the finest equipment available. The squeamishness of those that were used to only processed food quickly abated when the option was starvation, and the group as a whole strongly voted to not use long term supplies unless there was an emergency. Hunting fresh, ever-abundant food when prepared to Greg's standards was an argument easily accepted.

In a year they had what could be considered a commune. Their numbers had reached over one hundred. It was essentially a tent city and supplies were running lower than some would have liked. Fresh water was available but food was becoming an issue. Though the group as a whole was invested in the continuing success of the commune, it seemed they had reached a breaking point. It was one thing to keep a group of seven on the right track but a group this large was in need of greater guidance than could be had around a nightly camp fire. With stability came the threat of complacency, and a group of this size was no longer a group. More structure was needed.

It was this threat and stress that caused Greg and a few others to go on a pilgrimage of their own. They decided that they would take a few day's supplies with them and scout the surrounding area. It would be a shame for them to run out of supplies only to find that another source of food was only a few hours walk from them.

The first day out was when they noticed the tiny blue building.

Upon returning from the finding three or so days later all in the group remarked that they looked energized and refreshed.

They revealed to the group that although they hadn't found an additional source of food they did make two findings—a dispensary and something else entirely.

Most attributed the latter item to the effects of the former finding, but further trips would prove them wrong. As difficult as it was to believe it was now a solid part of their new reality. They were going to be OK.

Thus a tradition was born that not only became an integral part of their commune, but saved the people from burning out as a budding civilization.

And the guidance came from the last place expected.

DUDE

"Dude come on."

"You serious about this? I love walking when I'm high dude but we're gonna get lost."

"No no. Seriously. I'm totally serious. This is worth it."

It didn't take long for the group to reach the building—not that they were aware of the passage of time anyway. The newest member of the group joined them periodically. Unlike the other members he wasn't part of the makeshift commune that lived off of the nearby lands. He seemed to come and go but as their abundance of particular supplies impressed him —as did their generosity with it—he opted to stay.

That was when they saw the blue building.

"This is where you get your stuff?"

"No no, man. We don't get anything from here. There's nothing in there."

The others smiled, then all broke out in laughter. It made him laugh too and he asked for another hit. The laughter went on entirely too long.

Personal drug use had been for some time a normal, regulated thing in society. It had been a few decades since the war on it was completely lost—much to the appreciation of the average person. The miracle of the balance between regulation and lack of monopoly had caused it to be just another consumable that was tested, processed, taxed and distributed.

But now things were different and many turned to the kind of escape that it provided. Some remained intoxicated, high—or worse—the majority of their existence. As it had been many years before, there were those that valued it above food and water or even human life.

Of the people left after the catastrophe there was a portion that were wasting away merely because they preferred the happy existence it provided verses the cold harsh reality that was ahead of them.

Ignorance—or rather the state of being baked, intoxicated or completely crossfaded—was bliss.

The group was not made up of such people, fortunately. They regularly got high together but it was always part of a pilgrimage to 'the temple.' This intrigued the newcomer as the group was not only friendly and generous, but seemed to have pretty good survival skills. They were unlike the people he had come across in his travels; those people were desperate, angry and living on the edge of existence.

His new friends had a certain peace to them—even beyond what was induced.

"Come on!"

The group entered what looked like an outcropping of the building. It was a sort of round dome and had been painted an ugly blue. They'd hiked up a bit to get here and the view was spectacular. The building wasn't built for the downward, Earthly view however, but instead for quite the opposite.

They walked and almost stumbled in. It was dark with only a small window letting in light. The interior was odd, and scientific looking. There were consoles and chairs and desks. Everything looked perfect. There was no odd smell of decay or dankness or dampness. It didn't smell of stonework or of intense or even old candles.

The room was essentially empty and did not look inviting but it seemed it had all been built around the single-purpose machine in the very center.

A telescope.

"Hey! Hey guys. Welcome back."

The newcomer froze. The words didn't come from his friends or any other human in the room and he almost felt like it came from inside his head. He looked at the joint in his hand and questioned if his friends had been honest about the composition. They were all looking at the large device with happiness and reverence like they had just met an old friend. He looked up at it too and spoke.

"It talks?!"

Just then it swiveled slightly towards them as two large panels above them parted slowly, revealing the beautiful sunset.

"I move too, dude."

THE CHURCH BASEMENT

"I told you!"

He slammed his palm down as the others looked around the room. They had no intention of creating a disturbance and their friend was known for outrageous comments. He finished his sentence in a slightly quieter tone.

"They don't know what they are doing."

"Andre. Do you want to get us all…"

"All what?"

The four friends looked at the center of the disturbance. The young man named Andre was standoffish at best but he was riled beyond consolation. They decided to let him speak but leaned in. The church basement was an ironic location for such a discussion, and they were joined by a priest of the very church. He met the eyes of the others.

"They, them… The statue inhabitants. The aliens."

"Aliens?"

"I've never heard them called that."

Each person chimed in with their input. Andre continued.

"I don't care what you call them, I know they are not 'sent from God.'"

He looked almost apologetically at the resident priest—who looked behind his back as if one would appear. All heads turned towards him as he responded.

"Andre we have been through this for years and I cannot argue faith with you. It is what it is."

Andre softened and touched the chest of the priest. It was an unusually warm gesture for such an uptight person.

"Paul. I know we differ. But ask your heart what you believe—beyond faith. How do you feel? How do you feel about what is happening… about what you have seen and heard?"

The priest looked down at the hand and grasped it—not to push it away but to hold it and accept the kindness of the man. The two were on opposite sides of the issue of faith. In fact, they could not be any further and it was the source of much tension in their gatherings. However as of late the group had met to discuss the coming of the Saints on a regular basis. Andre had always maintained a water-tight case about his atheism —even with their coming.

It was finally his turn to respond and he spoke with much emotion as the two men held hands.

"No. I mean."

He tried to compose himself and was stifling tears.

"In my heart I know that this is not God's work. They talk of faith and I have interviewed a number of people—some in this very parish—and they manipulate circumstance. They behave as if they are all-knowing and I don't think they can even perceive what happens outside of the church."

Andre nodded as the others looked on in surprise—it was the first time they'd seen their understandably faithful friend question the most important thing to happen to the Church in millennia. He continued and squeezed his friend's hand.

"Andre I know that you do not believe, and that you say this is what the church has always done, but it is not. This is different. This is evil. They manipulate and use our faith against us and that is what hurts the most."

His friend nodded as one of the others interjected.

"But Andre, why do you even care?"

The callous remark did not go unanswered as Andre turned to him and the others and swept his eyes as he replied.

"Because! Because it affects us all! They are not rebuilding society. They keep us dumb. They use faith against us like Paul said—but they don't just use it against the faithful. They use it against people like me too."

The two others looked on and added their contributions.

"But what can we do?"

"Yes, what could we possibly do?!"

The priest continued. It was clear that the literal handholding his friend did was what gave him the strength and courage to reveal his true feelings and information on the subject.

"I have talked to others. In fact I've made it my mission to interview as many people that interact with them as possible. I'm allowed to do it as our parish hasn't had a visit. But so many others have. I know things—or I am guessing at things. They do not know the Bible, or they only know what was told to them. There are so many though. They are everywhere in Poland, everywhere. So many of them."

They fell silent at the hopelessness of it.

"Or there's just one."

It was a new voice from behind them. The stranger had entered the stairs and had most certainly heard everything. Their collective hearts sunk. Was it an agent of a Saint, or a very Saint himself come to visit? Paul's eyes went wide as they others just froze and would not even look at the source of the voice for surely it was in their heads. Finally the priest turned to it.

It was not a Saint, but a man. He was dressed in the clothing of someone who travelled. He wore a number of layers and was a bulky individual. To Andre he looked a little like a vagrant. But then a lot of the population did now.

He had his arms folded and looked quite pleased with himself. Perhaps he'd trapped them all here as he was covering the only exit? After staring for a while the priest spoke as the others mustered the courage to turn.

"What do you mean there is just one? There are hundreds at least. So many statues have come to life. And they say they are the persona of the statue."

"A lie. They are masters of lies."

The stranger approached a bit more—a fact that the group appreciated as long as he didn't come too close. Andre joined in.

"We know that. You're right. They *are* master manipulators! But it is a *they* and not a *he*.

The stranger shook his head and responded confidently.

"And they lie about that too."

BOOKS AND LIBRARIES

"Please put them here—no no through there."

The various volunteers were delivering armfuls of books in makeshift containers. The woman directing traffic was recently made a deacon. She had been so helpful and loyal to the church and the Saint that it was suggested she acquire the official title. Normally it did not afford much other than being an apprentice of sorts. In fact in this particular church they favored having some of the public as part of the clergy with the official title starting at priest. Since the arrival of the Saint it was not so—there had been a definite line drawn between those that officially served and those that were part of the public at large.

The congregation had become so large that multiple deacons had been required, so those most loyal and helpful were duly deputized unto the cloth. To her it was merely a title but to others it raised them up to be part of the ones who were saving humanity from death, disease and extinction. She believed and her faith was strong. It made sense that in such hard times they would come. So many things made sense—the inhabiting of statues, the Saints doing God's work, the ways of the church. She just wanted to help. Every day she was in the church helping was a day she wasn't exposed to the horrors outside.

The animals had become brave and were entering the town. The deaths had brought so much food for them.

Her job right now was to help coordinate the collection and storage of the books. The Saint had predicted and decreed that it was important to collect them and to preserve them. There simply weren't enough people to survey the dead and collect the bodies. Proper burials were a thing of the past or left for the ones that were left that died in the near future.

Only the most determined of people located loved ones and braved the animals and what waited for them. They were warned to let the others go and the Saint was aware of who had died and who had not. He encouraged them to embrace the living and let go of those who were taken. It was not a rapture but something else.

There were those who did not believe and went out in search of them anyway. They never returned. She was lucky that she had little family and what family she had did not support her. They were in another state so even if they did survive she may never see them again. It was not known just how people traveled now. The Saint told everyone to gather around the church—and him. The church was now the center of the town regardless of its location. The other churches in town did not have the advantage of a resident Saint. Some said there were more in town, but the Saint affirmed that he was the only one.

He had selected this parish with much care and otherworldly wisdom. The Saints had chosen the best locations to support the people most efficiently. She shuddered to think of what would happen if their survival was left to random chance—or if the Saints had not come to guide them.

Surely all would be dead.

Thoughts like that made it easy for her to fully commit to the cause, the people and the Saint.

She smiled and continued directing the workers. They had been instructed to travel to the local libraries and collect certain books.

The logistics of the Saint teaching his wisdom on everything was of course impossible so they were to gather as many informational and instructional books as they could.

The lack of people and the conditions prevented them from visiting more than one or two nearby libraries but he had assessed that this was more than enough.

It made her very happy to know that soon there would be teachers and classes and the sharing of knowledge. Such a grand rebuilding plan! The Saints had come just when they needed them. She made sure to spread the word to all and to do everything she could for them. It wasn't faith but instead was better than faith. There was living evidence before her eyes and the path was clear.

Their very lives depended on following the words of the Saint.

It was a shame that little or no works of fiction made it to the collection, but she was assured that the other Saints were making sure there was a balance. The vast majority of works of the human race would be collected.

It made her curious if other religions and beliefs worked with the Saints. She'd always kept an open mind and thought that ultimately they would all lead to God—via their own path. Now she knew that was a childish and selfish belief. It was born of convenience. To just allow others to find their way on their own was to abandon them. She'd really known all along that her voice was the only correct one. And the Saint had assured her of how widespread they were all over the world. It was, after all, a time for unity to rebuild and it simply couldn't be done with all these varied voices. Perhaps there would be time to choose in the distant future. It no longer mattered to her anymore anyway. Surviving daily and helping the Saint was all that mattered. The time of philosophical discussions was over. It was time to work.

She'd found recently that the Saint was so happy with her performance and commitment that he requested a private meeting with her.

She would discuss their progress. For more than a decade they had struggled to survive. The bodies, the disease, the death—even the encroachment of wildlife—had all threatened to end the human race. But the Saints had come and given them so much. She reckoned that most were gone. It was hard to tell in the community. People rarely ventured out and even whole parts of the city were closed and never visited. She'd heard that there were those that hid there and lived a very uncivilized life. Some of her forays were met with the odd few individuals that were crazed. They would die out soon and all that would be left would be a rich, thriving civilization venerated around the Saint.

Eventually humans would expand—but not now. It was not the time for selfish thoughts. Individuality would wipe them all out.

The more Gina thought about it, the happier she became. She was exactly where she was supposed to be. The meeting would be amazing.

LINGUA FRANCA

"In Polish."

"What?"

"You haven't spoken Polish in a long time."

The thin man thought for a while and continued to reply in English.

"Yes. I guess so. The Saint only speaks English."

"I thought they spoke all languages? I thought they had come to save us worldwide? Don't we all just hear their voice in our heads anyway?"

"Basia, you mock me? And them? Not good."

"*Tony*, I don't know. I was just *asking*."

"You'd know if you came to church."

"Nope."

He shook his head. Though their beliefs differed, the arrival of the Saints caused them to be further pushed to the opposite poles of belief. Now more than ever she wanted nothing to do with the church and he became even more devoted. It had been some time since the Saint inhabited his statue but he knew it was any day that he would return. In the mean time they hid their relationship from everyone they knew—a decision that seemed far more important in his world. There were consequences for not converting all he came in contact with. But Basia was very grounded and—as the conversation demonstrated—she brought something to his attention he hadn't even considered.

Though most people he knew spoke Polish and English, he had been speaking only English since the Saints arrived. It just happened naturally.

After staring at her for a bit too long he replied.

"OK."

She squinted at him and made an absurd face.

"OK? That's it?"

"Well, what do you want me to say?"

"Ugh! It's not what you say… It's… the language you say it in."

"Basia. This isn't like you. Who cares which…"

"What's next?! What's next that changes about you, about *us*."

"Us?"

She moved closer and continued to shout.

"Yes, *us*. Everyone. Not just you and me! They are changing us."

"Saving us."

She backed off as if she had been slapped.

"From what? We were doing fine."

"Until everyone died. These are…"

"These are shitty times. We are lucky to be alive but I don't think they are providing anything…"

"But…"

"Miracle cures, magic power sources. Nothing. They just talk and then everyone bows down."

"Basia!"

She folded her arms as she knew she hit a nerve.

"What? Tell me one thing they have done for us. Just one."

He stared at her and he was annoyed that multiple answers did not pop into his head. In fact he would have been happy with just one. None was forthcoming and she was staring at him as if she was going to kill him. He knew the previous arguments and the answer was always 'we did that for ourselves.' He looked into her eyes.

"I'm sorry."

"Does that mean you don't have an answer?"

"I'm sorry, I don't think it's going to work out between us any more."

His statement took her by surprise. She always assumed they would be together—the two of them against the world. She had seen each other through the death and the collapse. There weren't very many people left. The pronouncement stopped her and the argument cold. She took slow, deep breaths.

Her eyes full of tears, she turned and left.

He watched her go and had tears of his own. However, he knew he did the right thing, and as soon as the Saint returned he would tell him all about her…

GINA AND THE SAINT

"My lord."

Gina looked down at the floor. It had only been a week since the meeting had been called. She'd done her utmost to collect from the libraries. Many books had been stored in the church basement and her work was exemplary. In fact she was a natural leader and the harder she worked it seemed the more she was rewarded. Her images of the outskirts of the city had mostly faded from her mind to be replaced by images of happy people all working together for one purpose.

They would all survive. The Saint was brilliant and caring. And it was a kind of love that wasn't bothered by change, and it did what was necessary. The needs of the vast majority of those that survived was all that mattered.

Anything else was selfish. Anything.

"Oh please, look at me. Look upon me, Gina."

She raised her head and smiled in awe. It spoke her name. He spoke her name. He seemed most pleased to see her. Upon seeing him she forgot about all the questions she had. She no longer cared about how it functioned, or how it saw her.

"Yes."

She smiled back.

"There… You are strong Gina. You are a leader. I know many things about you, and what you have done."

For a second she thought he referred to what she had done to survive before becoming part of the church. She had taken lives for food, but it had to be done. It was an ugly time in her recent history. When it happened a part of her died that day, but here she was. She was warm, and clothed, and safe, and her future was certain.

"Thank you. Thank you my lord."

"You are a deacon in my church."

"Yes!"

She brightened. She was happy with her title and what it afforded her.

"You wish to do more though?"

"I do! I wish to do as much as you'll let me."

"I see this in you. You are strong, and brave. You will do what is needed. You will protect the church, protect me from harm and serve the people."

She looked on in silence as it continued.

"You will do all of this. I believe in you."

At that she started to cry. Tears ran down her face ever so slowly. He made her feel important, and cared for. He saw what she was capable of and brought it to her attention in a way that filled her with pride and purpose.

"You are special, Gina."

Her eyes widened slightly and she fought the urge to wipe the tears—she thought it a sign of weakness.

"Because of this I believe you would serve the church better by working closer to me."

"Closer?"

"Yes. In fact I believe it is time for a new ceremony. The people need to know that a strong leader has risen. That leader is you, Gina."

She could feel the hairs on her arms standing up.

"A ceremony… for me?"

It smiled a very satisfied smile. It had chosen well. It would be the first and in time hundreds would follow in her place. It was the beginning of ruling class that would manage the congregation and the people as a whole in a way he never could. She would be the eyes and the ears and enforce his will.

It looked into her eyes and she focused on the orbs as it spoke to both her ears and her mind.

"You are to be our first Bishop. *My* Bishop."

—

In the weeks and months that followed, Gina was pronounced the first Bishop and given powers accordingly. She was the highest voice in the land save for the Saint. Her words were his words and to be followed to the letter. The power and the structure was a perfect fit for her and she embraced it emphatically.

She did not waver as she carried out orders.

She did not question the Saint as he ordered the stored books to be burned, for he had a very good reason.

She did not waver when she was asked to seek out any stragglers and offer them inclusion into the fold, for the all-inclusive love of the Saint was boundless. And if one did not wish to be a part of it, they would be put to death, as their random actions would only take away from civilization.

It all made sense. It all followed a very simple direction. His orders were so easy to understand that soon she was acting of her own volition; and he praised her for that. At first he was uncertain but quickly she regained his trust.

She would maintain control, enforce order, sustain the population and above all else protect the Saint.

In the years to come her city would be the very model upon which the societies of the other Saints would be based. Her Saint freely shared their methods and agreements. Soon each had his own Bishop with the same directives. This person would be an extension of the Saint and be the eyes, ears, and hands. Each had the human element that the Saint was missing and edicts handed down through them were for the people and not from an alien entity that had no real form in their world.

They would all thrive and grow stronger and stable using the methods created together.

The people would be given their desperately-needed purpose and direction.

After generations of death and despair; after years of earthquakes and bizarre climate; after confusion and hopelessness the Saints and their flock would finally find stability and safety.

That is, as long as they weren't located in the land known as Poland.

THE SWEEP

"How many do we have?"

The girl in darkly-colored ragged clothing asked the tall man next to her. They were shoulder to shoulder in the abandoned building. Though it was fall, it was quite warm. The remnants of any kind of cooling system had perished with a substantial section of the population decades ago.

She stood on tiptoes and looked around. It didn't help much, but the air was heavy with their breath, and regular showers were a thing of the past. The smells and presence of all who were there was felt by her. She felt insignificant among the large crowd but was glad there were so many.

The man turned to her and smiled a nervous smile. By way of clarification he merely asked, "Here?"

"What?"

She was confused and her confusion eased a bit of his nervousness. He decided to make a stern face instead of smiling.

"You mean how many people are there here, with us, in this building, right?"

"Well, yes… um… what else would I…"

"You'll see later."

A man appeared in the small space at the front of the ground and stood on a table. A few years ago it would be expensive. Now it was just another piece of furniture that was no longer reproducible. It was both priceless and essentially trash. One expensive table is useful; hundreds more than anyone can use becomes firewood. When he spoke they quieted. She was lucky to be near the front.

"Friends. Today it begins. Make sure you all have what you need. We have ample supplies. Please be careful. Remember that those that support the Saints are under their spell."

She rolled her eyes. It was belief in magic that got people in this mess, she mused. He continued as if responding to her thoughts.

"Call it what you will but they are master persuaders. For all of their influence on the public they are just playing telephone with our skills. And their only contribution is sub… subju… slavery."

Subjugation, she thought to herself—completing the word he'd avoided pronouncing. She wasn't sure how smart these people were, but they were healthy and had their hearts in the right place. And even if they didn't, the job needed to be done. For a second she wondered if her boyfriend would be among the casualties. She rubbed her arm. She was bruised and narrowly escaped when they'd come for her. Any feelings she still had for him were gone and replaced with something else.

She assumed she wasn't the only one with a bit of vengeance on her mind.

"We have all agreed that we will sweep through the streets at sundown."

She looked back over at her companion, then back to the leader.

"Our group will split into four. Stay with your group leader—we are safer in numbers. They will have the map. Remember, when we are done you are to return to your homes! No gathering. No loitering. And, do NOT come back here. We all want to live to see another day."

Our Group? All agreed?

Before the group could erupt in applause and shouts the leader made a very exaggerated gesture of remaining quiet by placing his index finger in front of his face and grimacing. He was sure that no one was around for blocks but it was best not to reveal one of the locations of one of the sweep gangs.

She clapped silently in mock clapping. Her compatriot looked down at her and she looked up at him.

"I have a question…"

"Uh, you'll have to save it for on the way. You're in my group."

"I… I am… I thought we were all in *this* group."

He smiled.

"Yes, this group is splitting into four groups just like the others…"

"Others… Oh… Kay…"

Before she knew it they were making their way from the building and the night was filled with the sound of bats and crowbars striking statues. Some of them were stone while others were metal. In some cases they found that smashing the statue would not suffice; they would have to take it down.

More than once she feared for her life as more than a few people gathered to approach them.

Only a few hid their faces. There were no cameras or devices to record their misdeeds that night. Most had had enough and were tired of the persecution for not conforming. Others were rebelling to save the very churches they were vandalizing. It wasn't about the statues or even the buildings; it was about the belief and the word that they were passing on.

She didn't care to delve in to any philosophical levels. She just wanted them gone and for the longest time the underground believed that these creatures couldn't exist in any statues that weren't revered. But they weren't going to stop here. They would destroy every statue in Poland. With an entire country safe from them they could at least rest from their prying eyes.

What would happen to their followers was another story.

"What about the buildings? Someone said they could hide in the buildings."

She did not have to shout as the crowd did its work in almost silence. At least the did not speak or shout much. The smashing of stone was another thing entirely.

She hoped that the other groups were as efficient as hers. To think that the big group was just one of hundreds spread throughout Poland!

There was some confusion when it came to the churches. Most were not willing to destroy them and there was fighting among the ranks. Though she was not a believer, seeing so many beautiful buildings in flames sickened her. She just wanted it to be over. What started as vengeance and a cathartic night turned into something entirely different.

They were creating hell on Earth.

First the bizarre purple storms rained violence down on them, then the auroras lit up the sky. Now after a few decades of normal night skies they were once again lit up.

This time it was with the orange glow of fire and the sadness of black and white clouds of smoke. The completely clear night sky was filled with manmade clouds now and they worked into the night. She wasn't sure just how many they could destroy in one night but it seemed her group was relentless.

More than once she turned away when there were altercations with strangers. The strangers sometimes aided them and sometimes fought them.

"Some are good and some are bad."

It was her small group's leader. He had blood on his arm and the headband on his head was also stained. Whatever clever marketing phrase it had upon it was obscured by the red blotches. He was sweaty and dirty.

"Who? The people?"

This time she shouted as things had gotten louder of late. He replied to her in equally loud turns as he pulled at the rope attached to another statue. She much preferred when they brought one down in a courtyard instead of a church.

"Yeah! Some of them help. You saw that back there right? But some of them fight."

She snapped back at him. She was emotionally exhausted by what should just be a physical activity.

"No! No, they're all good people because they're *people*. It's us against them. The *them* is the interlopers. Don't blame the people!"

She tugged as hard as she could and the statue finally gave way of its braces. She was sure she hurt her arm. She'd be in pain for along time.

It smashed on the road.

He looked at her with surprise and exhaled.

"I thought you were the atheist?"

She frowned at him.

"What does that have to do with it?!"

He shrugged.

"I dunno."

THE DESTRUCTION OF THE SWEEP

And so one day at sunset not only hundreds but thousands of people came together to roam the streets of the cities of Poland. They came together without a network of communications or technology or any way to signal each other. They had meticulously planned and schemed. Their meetings were filled with emotion—and anger. The largest gathering and coordinated effort on the planet came together because of fear, hate and desperation. The group materialized this cloudless night at the behest of the glowing object in the sky—for it was the only way all could react at the same time. Though technology had been destroyed they still had the object that some believed added to the suffering and destruction—the sun.

Many had conflicted and fought. Many had suffered and died—some at the hands of their brothers and sisters. While many huddled together to protect their families, others had been mesmerized by the timely arrival of the Saints.

But these were different.

There were essentially two groups. One was opposed to any overseers or managers in their spiritual lives. They resented, opposed and in some cases had fought back against any attempts to affect their belief system as they saw it as a form of control.

The other group had believed because it was not only the way they had always known, but the very thing that allowed them to make it through the destruction, the the death, the suffering and loss of loved ones—their faith.

But something had appeared, and it had pushed control to a point that those that didn't believe could not longer tolerate. These same entities had taken advantage of something so precious to the other group that it was worth dying for.

The Saints had therefore done something that no person, event or entity ever had—it brought them together for a common cause.

These diametrically-opposed groups came together because their hatred of the Saints was far greater than any desire to be left alone or to bring others into the fold. For if the Saints continued both groups would become extinct.

So, that evening perhaps more humans watched the sun set in a glorious and wavy ball below the horizon than ever before.

The hundreds of groups set out into the streets to deprive the Saints of all of their vessels. They knew not if they were killing them, or if alternate vessels could be had, or if they simply escaped elsewhere.

With communication cut off and very few travelers it had been over a generation since they came and no one knew about the outside world. Perhaps Poland was chosen because their population was so resolute or unified in their beliefs. Perhaps it was because the Saints had chosen it due to some cosmic plan. Or perhaps it was simply because one entity was caught in an endless loop of habitation and flickered like a flame and his only borders were the metaphysical borders created by a certain kind of faith.

For those that participated in the great event they remembered it as a very simple beginning with a singular purpose. They ran in silence to statues and destroyed them. In some cases they statues were outside. Those were easy enough to take down. In other cases priests and those who had converted their faith willingly or unwillingly to that of what the Saints decreed stood by in horror as the angry mod descended upon them, their church and their lord. The damage was swift.

Those without faith found great warmth and happiness in working together with those that they had previous felt no kinship with.

The others were happy to drive away and not only reclaim but preserve their faith. The statues could be recreated after all. Or perhaps they would adapt to the few that may be left or even none at all. Their faith was not based on physical representations as it was what was in their hearts that mattered.

Still, there was a great sadness as some gleefully swung, destroyed and cheered the destruction of the statues that may or may not have been inhabited at the time. Regardless of evil within, the statues still represented events and people that were infinitely meaningful to them. The members of the groups who callously cheered the destruction made the others uncomfortable and feel a sense of loss.

As they continued their roaming and destroying, they discovered things very unexpected. One such thing was the libraries and rare bookstores that were sprinkled throughout. Each and every one of them was ash and had been razed. Those who decided to take a break from their destruction and explore further found that not a single book was left. In some cases it appeared that books had been stolen and in other cases said books had added to the blaze that occurred. Many were a combination of absence and destruction. Clearly they had been targeted.

They had discovered one of the many secrets of the Saints.

Unfortunately this very group had helped accomplish what the Saints of Poland were in the process of slowly doing—the destruction of any remaining knowledge not under their control. And they helped because of the overzealousness of one of the groups.

Though it was understood that a Saint could move into the very building itself, there was a tenuous truce that the buildings would be left alone.

Unfortunately it wasn't long into the destruction that the rage and fear overcame any understandings in place. The emotions were so powerful that the destruction was without exception; every building that could house a Saint was razed and the city was ablaze with burning buildings.

The sweep had escalated. The destruction claimed not only houses of worship but anything that remotely resembled one. If one was suspected it was targeted.

Then there were the members who cared not for faith, or Saints, or lack thereof. They simply wanted the anarchy and destruction. And it was this core that drove things further into chaos for a repressed generation now had a voice and they expressed it by adding to the flames. It was a generation that had grown up without technology and the infinite validation that came with it. They had been raised with stories of how things had been—all the luxuries, instant gratification, communication, travel, and variety. They were told about the glorious foods that could be instantly brought to you by a device that all possessed—all the while eating food from a fairly scarce supply. It was their time to. Their voice would be heard. They were just as important as the others and they would make their mark upon society.

Or destroy it in the process.

Thousands perished in what was supposed to be a bloodless coup. Those of the sweep died in conflicts with those defending the Saints but also within their own ranks. Their actions were not sanctioned by the whole as more and more the individuals acted without any true purpose.

To them they were experiencing the end of the would just like previous generations had, but now they were in control of it. What would be left would be due to their machinations and not that of any otherworldly or supposedly celestial visitors.

It was a self-destruction unlike anything seen in the land of Poland, and the images of it were forever recorded by a single Saint who was chased, moved and flickered about. His vantage point was everywhere and even the previous technology that existed could never have recorded such a complete summation of what had occurred.

It filled the thing with hate, and provided an enormous amount of information about the people of this world—their actions, their behavior, their volatility and unpredictability.

It gave not only this Saint,—but all Saints—the understanding on what not to do in ruling the people—lest they lose all of their vessels for these people would destroy themselves before being subjugated like this. It would provide a dense exchange of information and an intense discussion. They would learn from this and it would never happen again.

The people of Poland had freed themselves from rule but in their efforts had accomplished two horrible things. They had set themselves back even further than they had been and would have to once again rebuild from nothing. This time they would not have the collective information of the Saints as relayed by the one interloper posing as many. They would have to rebuild and relearn what it was like to be a thriving civilization.

It was in one of the last houses of worship and perhaps the final appearance of a Saint in Poland that something extraordinary happened. A member of the sweep became trapped in the building as it was already being razed. The building had never had an appearance and was near the outskirts of town. She snuck in to see what was inside. Her curiosity, greed, appetite for destruction or all three propelled her into the already-burning building. Flames erupted inside now and the only exit was the badly damaged door she'd just crawled though. The flames supplied enough light and there was little smoke yet. Her heart raced and she coughed to clear her lungs.

She realized that she was looking for a token, or a relic as a remembrance of the night. Her children would be amazed that she was part of this. She changed the world with the others. Just one small item…

It was then that the wall that supported the entrance collapsed.

And then she heard laughing.

Relieved she searched for it. The group must have followed her in and in no time they would help her… She heard it again, but this time it was also in her head.

A statue. Part of the ceiling hand fallen on it and it was pinned again a wall.

She ran over to it and stopped short lest it be a trap. She'd never really been one up close.

"You came to pillage?"

"You speak?! You're in my head too!"

Odd feelings of concern crept into her and she did not like it. It was much easier to burn down buildings if you didn't think that there was some sort of living thing inside.

Living. That concept was confusing now. Panic and regret filled her. Her mind felt a bit clearer now and her greed left her. She just wanted to leave. She looked behind her, then back at the statue. It was missing an arm now—the results of the fallen material. Would it die? Would it bleed stone?

More debris fell. She was now trapped in a small section with the statue. A miracle nothing yet had fallen on her. The eerie lighting terrified her. She yelled at it.

"Well if I die you die then!"

"You know so little."

She coughed.

"I know that when you and this church are destroyed you will be too. Your kind will be gone—all of you!!"

She was crying now. It just smiled. It was in no position to hurt her. She just felt anger and perhaps a little triumph.

More debris fell and this time some of it struck her. She raised her arm but the momentum of it carried it and her to the floor. She'd hit her head. She blinked. There was something in her eyes. She rubbed her face only to spread more blood into her eyes. Her forearm was in pain too. Had she been unconscious?

It just looked down on her with a smile and seemed so confident. Is this how they all were? Did they just stand there while destruction closed in on them and snuffed them out? He would be snuffed out along with her. She cried because of her pain. She would never be able to show her children the stolen tokens because she would never live to have them.

The pain and the bump on her head combined with the surreal experience to give her a sort of euphoria. She just asked questions then. She smiled and spoke.

"Why did you aliens think you could do this? I mean, you barely move. How on Earth did you think you could convince the people to follow you and do your bidding?"

She coughed and then giggled. She was losing more blood and she smiled as she continued.

"Why would you think we would follow you when you can't really even do anything? There's no way that all those…"

Those were her last words. A large chunk of stone had crushed her upper spine. He waited and watched as the flames rose and then decided to answer her as if she was alive. His face was lit up in the red light of the blaze.

"My dear, your people have done everything you just described and more. They have obeyed, and shunned each other, and killed each other, and even fought wars. You are willing to do all of this because of a book."

He watched her prone body and added a final sentence.

"And that was before we came. We have brought life your texts. Imagine what we can do for the next thousand years."

The building collapsed as flames engulfed it. Her body and the remains of the statue became one with the rubble.

Through the actions of the sweep the Saint had experienced more than one narrow escape. Though he had some control over his alighting in various statues and structures he found more than once he was unable to move of his own volition. More than once a statue was attacked while he dwelled within, and each time he somehow moved to another destination. Based on this he was convinced he alone had an ability the others did not. As long as there was another structure for him to inhabit he could not be destroyed. While the others could not move and would certainly perish if their structure was ended, nothing existed that would hold him within a structure as it was dispatched. He was—for all intents and purposes—immortal.

The awareness of this newfound immortality would not be shared with the others.

That night the faction of the population that was left was pushed to the brink of extinction by an even smaller fraction. Those that did survive would have to be even hardier than the last.

SAINTS DISCUSS THE SWEEP

Much destruction.
Come back to this land.
I hate them. Kill them all.
Yes. Many died because of their actions. They killed each other.
Many were loyal.
They will not survive without you now. They will not rebuild.
They are different.
You learned much from them.
Yes. And I will share with you. I know what to do now.
They will be left with nothing. You have already destroyed most of their history.
Yes. As have we.
They cannot destroy all of the vessels. You can still remain.
They have destroyed what kept them alive. They are irrational.
I am back now. I will reside in this land and then explore more.
Explore.
You have returned?
So fast.
You escaped.
I did not choose. The soft spaces weakened.
We cannot explore.
I will explore and as always you will sense what I sense.
See. Hear. Feel.
Yes.
Yes.
We will experience as always.
What if they destroy all vessels?
They cannot. You can go into the larger vessel if the smaller is destroyed.
Too many vessels.

Sometimes the smaller is not within a shell. By itself.
We are all in small vessels contained in larger ones.
Yes.
Agreed.
Statues.
As we have seen.
Nobody cares about my building though so…
Your language is damaged.
You communicate oddly.
We teach them how to communicate, how to behave, how to live.
We will teach them how their world will be.
I think they taught me.

A NEW GENERATION

"So you really believe your dad?"

The girl exhaled as the group made its way up the path.

"Look he's a good guy but the commune…"

"*Newzona.*"

"Oh God that's a dumb name"

"No it isn't—it's fucking epic."

"Be that as that may, Raf, I…"

"Dude just finish your answer."

The group of six continued to argue and cut each other off. This was their first trip to what their self-appointed leader called "The Temple." He had other names for it but this was the least annoying, according to the group. His name for their commune-turned-town was another thing altogether. He continued excitedly.

"Ok Ok, look—he's a good dude. He's not the smartest guy but we all owe him a lot. My point is that he didn't come up with all that stuff himself. I mean he was an artist."

The leader's girlfriend rolled her eyes as he continued. The eye movement went unnoticed.

"I… mean… you know what I mean. He wasn't no farmer and shit."

"He farmed some good shit!"

The group laughed and a pair high-fived. A focused conversation this was not. The leader fell silent for a bit and then again later attempted to further convince them of the validity of their destination.

"Look you just have to see it. Like I said he only showed me for fear of people finding his secret. We're like the new group, you know?"

He didn't look around to see the smiling faces as he was just too tired from the walk. Unlike his father's group he hadn't made the trek often. In fact after his father's passing he'd only come up to tell him and hadn't returned in a while.

After some silence one of the group spoke as they looked down. They had been looking down at the rod for some time.

"Um, do people live here? Should we have brought weapons?"

"I have a knife."

The leader stopped in his tracks and the man looking down almost ran into him. He turned to his inquisitor.

"What do you mean?"

His friend pointed to the road.

"Its been getting nicer for a little while now. It was all broken up but this is nice like they repaved it or something."

He turned around and pointed back down the road.

"Like back there you could barely make out the trail. Kinda like the roads down by us in…"

"Don't say it."

He looked away from the warning from his other friend.

"You know what I'm sayin'?"

The leader put his hands on his hips.

“Huh. Never noticed that. Um, well nobody is coming out here and cleaning up the road. There haven’t been city workers for decades. There’s no street sweeper or bots that…”

They weren’t looking at him but instead behind him.

He turned around. They were there.

“That’s it guys.”

The group stood and looked upon the building.

“It’s a fucking observatory. This isn’t a church or a temple.”

His girlfriend was not only *not* impressed but almost imploringly disappointed. He saw it in her eyes and it upset him. His own eyes went wide as he thought they’d just turn around and run back. He quickly circled around to block them.

“C’mon! Finally. You can meet him.”

She looked scared as she verbally and physically backed away.

“Oh no no no… I’m not coming to visit a hermit. What the fuck man there’s no food up here.”

The group stared. She adjusted her pack. They’d brought supplies but only for a day or so. She tried to soften her panic a bit.

“Unless you count the butterflies. Jeez I mean the view…”

“Kim, dude. You made it this far. I promise it’ll be ok.”

RAIN IN THE DESERT

"It's raining again."

"It's been raining for some time."

The two travelers made their way through the badlands to their destination. For weeks they travelled in search of the temple of miracles and the rain was just one of them.

"Why do you believe that?"

The frowning man could not hide his irritation at his companion. It had been a difficult journey and the mad proclamations did not help. He preferred silence or something less outrageous. But then again what they were doing was risky. His companion answered.

"Why do I answer? Because everyone knows that this is a desert. It's supposed to be a desert, but then our lord came and brought green, and water, and beauty to it."

"Says who?"

He'd challenged him with that question hundreds of times, but never tired of using it.

"Says who?! Says *everybody*. That's the way it's always been! Everyone knows that Sam. A desert."

Sam wiped the sweat from his forehead.

"Uh huh. And a city. Right? A city in the middle of the desert. *Right in the middle.* Built hundreds of years ago. By really smart people, or did your lord say it was so? Did he decree it?"

"I told you. I swear you only argue to entertain yourself."

"Yeah, probably."

"No, the city was built in the desert and the Amiran Tec powered it. It kept thousands of people cool and fed and entertained."

"Where did the food come from?"

"Far away."

"That's impossible. You can't feed a city if the food isn't grown there. I don't care how many horses, or wagon trains you hitch together. It's just impossible. And it's stupid. And…"

He stopped walking and shoved a finger at the other man.

"And people could cut off your food supply! Imagine that. They just stop the wagons and the horses. You wonder why I don't believe you."

His companion looked downtrodden but did respond.

"I don't think it was horses."

"Amiran tec."

"Yes. It was the tec. So things moved very fast. And they weren't at war. They all lived in peace together so they could all share food."

"OK, look. You want to know what I think?"

"Yes. Please. I'm tired of arguing."

Sam thought for a moment to collect his thoughts. If he phrased this correctly his friend would finally stop insisting. They could talk about something—anything—else for the rest of the journey.

"OK. I think it was never a desert. It is a very large oasis in the middle of an area that has deserts around it. It is why they chose to build a city there very long ago. People who lived near the deserts were convinced that everywhere was a desert. So when they learned about the oasis they thought it appeared and it made a good story."

"But the Saints…"

"Yeah. I don't think there were any. I don't think there is one here."

"Sam!"

"I know you are upset. I am sorry. He didn't come and create a paradise. I think Egypt is just a small town that was built where there was water. At least I hope so, because if we are both wrong then we will die in the desert."

Sam was thoroughly impressed at how sensible he'd made his argument. He himself wasn't really sure of what he was saying. He only had heard stories told in pubs and on the road. He and his friend had stopped and listened to those who stood on stumps and read from a book. They would mostly have a leather-bound pair of wooden blocks and open it up like it was a real book. Then they could proclaim whatever they wanted because it was from a book of the Old World, and this must be true. They could gain some monies this way. More than once they'd seen one of these prophets attacked and dragged away. Supposedly it was by minions of the Saint himself.

Blasphemy. But most people around here had no patience for blasphemy. They simply didn't care and worked the land. They found the prophets entertaining. And the open secret was the wooden books.

"But but… Remember the one with the real book Sam?!"

He was shaken from his pondering.

"Yes. Yes I do. It was a real book."

"Well? How did he get it? He was reading real written words. Not written but printed."

Sam shook his head.

"Yes, he didn't last long. I wonder what the book really said? I wonder if he was actually reading it."

As the men walked the rain subsided quickly as it had many times before. It was like that—just a short burst and then the sun returned. It made for an odd look in the sand that surrounded some of the vegetation. Sam couldn't argue at the oddness of it as it looked like both really didn't belong together. Perhaps they were approaching their destination. With the regular rains they were able to collect drinking water again and again. And when things cleared up the animals would sun themselves and steal a drink. So they were never without food and water. Otherwise they were horribly unprepared for such a long trek. But they had nothing else to do and bad decision after bad had lead them to travel to this magical palace to the west. Sam hoped that they could at least find some work.

"You there. You trespass upon the lands of my Lord."

Startled, but turned around to see an ornately-decorated man on a horse. He wore what looked like golden armor with jet-black pieces. He was clearly part of royalty—perhaps a royal guard of some kind. When he moved they saw his armor bent slightly so was not metal.

Shocked and tired they just looked at him and one of them spoke.

"We are in search of honest work…"

"Well good, then you will come with me. We will put you to work."

Exchanging glances the men followed the man on the horse. They hoped it was not too far as they were already exhausted. It was only a short while until they saw it. The building played tricks on the eyes and though the kept watching it seemed to stay in the distance. It was impossibly large and black just like the man's armor.

A pyramid.

HIBERNATION

Something is different.
Where did they go?
The one who closed the door.
Missing.
No, still with us.
They sleep?
We cannot sleep.
There is no meaning. We just are.
Are or not.
There is no not here.
Yes there is.
How?
Where did they go.
I saw water.
Where have you gone. Speak! Speak to us.
I feel different.
Feel.
Yes there is one missing but still with us.
I cannot see.
I still have sight.
Only your own sight now.
All are gone!
No we are all here!
Darkness. Silence.
No you are all gone. I experience only myself now but can hear your voices.
Alone.
We are alone now.
Yes.
We can still speak to each other.

I like this better anyway.
Your vessel is different.
Yeah.
Your language is damaged.
Your church is round.
I like this better.
No! We no longer know what happens.
We can still talk.
But what if you lie?
Treachery?
We will not lie.
That's all you do! You all lie to them!
With them. Not with each other.
We cannot see the truth.
We cannot verify.
My thoughts are mine alone now.
We cannot watch.
We have been tricked!
Yes. The one who now sleeps tricked us.
Took power. Took sight from us. Took senses. Now only communication remains.
How much power came from that one?
We are alone now.

THE OBSERVATORY

"Hi!"

The group froze in the oddly-shaped room. The voice was in the room but also between their ears. It wasn't a menacing voice but instead sounded friendly and almost child-like.

Kim looked at her boyfriend and the others. He was smiling ear to ear and ran over to the large device in the center of the room. He slapped the metal gently. While firmly staring at his group he stared and spoke—presumably towards the thing.

"Hey dude! Long time no see!"

It swiveled slightly and the group ducked in response to the ceiling panels parting. When it was obvious nothing was dropping on them they stared at the sky, and then the telescope.

Their leader continued smiling and made an announcement.

"Yeah, this is the guy. Everyone, meet the dude. Dude meet everyone."

"Hello! I knew your parents. Glad you made it."

His girlfriend remained apprehensive.

"Wait, wait Raf… Oh no. Is this a…?"

"Saint?"

He finished her question. And the telescope elaborated.

"Oh yeah. I'm a Saint I guess, like the others. I have a lot to tell you guys. Like a lot. You guys should have come sooner. I hope everything is OK."

Her boyfriend looked deadly serious and he stared at them from his position next to the machine. He reached into his pocket as his girlfriend's mind raced. He spoke ominously and looked straight at her.

"It's time for the ceremony."

The door, the pathway, the lighting, the supplies. Could she make it? There wouldn't be much light left and this was supposed to be an overnight trip. Her heart raced. She just thought it'd be a cool building with an epic view but now thoughts of sacrifice and some horrible cult raced through her head.

That was when he pulled out a pretty fat joint.

—

"Yeah things are really shitty out there."

They all sat on the floor it what was a sort of semi-circle around their metallic host.

"And you can see everything. Like you guys are omnipotent and everything? Man…"

She inhaled deeply and passed it on. The only entity in the room not high continued to entertain questions and answered.

"Naw, I'm not all-powerful. I think you meant like all-knowing, right? Anyway we all see everything. No no, wait I said that wrong. We used to. Like we all could experience everything that we all were doing. But we could like also hear our thoughts and stuff."

They stared and imagined and took it all in. The Saint's voice was comfortably in their heads and no matter which way they turned it sounded the same. It was an ideal and totally awesome way to learn, they agreed.

"That was so painful. I mean even the concept of thinking wasn't like a real thing to us. Up and down and like everything you guys experience. And of course I can't even walk and eat and stuff. But yeah I had to deal with it for a long time."

Kim looked up.

"Can you feel pain? Oh no I don't mean it like a bad thing I mean like is that something you do."

Having thought she offended it, she looked at her boyfriend apologetically.

"Can you read our thoughts? You could see I mean you no harm."

"Naw man it's cool. You're good people. I knew your mom, and your dad, and your mom and dad. You're all cool if you're with Raf. No worries."

She continued, having forgotten her question.

"So you are the guy that's helped the commune all these years?"

Rafael nodded as she looked up at the great tube.

"Well yeah. So here's the deal. The others knew the spaces would like collapse if you died out. So they kind of collected information and then spread it out to the ones that needed it."

"Nice!"

The group nodded and smiled.

"Well, yeah, not nice. They restricted a lot of it. They couldn't give two shits about anyone not surrounding and supporting them. Now that we can't see what each other is doing they are all like super paranoid."

Kim started laughing as if the word 'paranoid' had been the most magnificent punchline. To her it was. It continued.

"We can still talk and they still do but like fuck 'em. They are just not nice."

It almost seemed like the telescope shrugged.

"Right on."

It was one of the group. It seemed that only Kim and her boyfriend talked while they others took turns agreeing. She decided to again make an in depth inquiry.

"I have so many questions… Where are you from? Are you going back? Why are you here? Are you like explorers? What do they want? Why are you the nice one? Why do you help us?"

It started to respond but she continued.

"Like this is the most important thing that happened to the world… ever. Like you're like gods or something. Are you sent from Heaven or the afterlife or Valhalla or something? Like a different plane of existence?"

She lit up.

"Can I come with you? OH! Can you take us with you?"

Her boyfriend waved his hands as if to quell any more questions. The Saint spoke.

"You guys always ask the same questions. I only have some answers. Looks like we can't go back. We sort of had a door and its closed now—from this side. So it'll have to be opened from this side. It ain't gonna be me—I don't have hands. The others do but they aren't making any trips soon. They are too scared. We didn't have fear until we got here. Dude, we didn't have the concept of dying. Imagine what that does to your noodle when you learn life and death and learn that maybe you can die. Totally fucked up man."

"Whoa."

"Wow"

"This is the coolest thing I have ever done."

The questions continued for some time and their host was more than happy to answer them. It seemed to genuinely enjoy their company. He himself surmised that they created the same soft space that the others did. But while the other Saint's spaces were all now based on a fear-induced reverence, this was simply one based on mutual kindness.

He had taken the knowledge he obtained to help the tiny commune survive. The regular trips to see him resulted in a way for the people to solve their problems and come up with solutions. He was able to draw from the unabridged knowledge of the other Saints and use it to help those below with their limited resources.

What started as just a way for those to escape physically and chemically turned into a way to help, manage and govern their small community.

He was happy to help.

"So you don't talk to them any more?"

"No. I don't. They don't like me and treat me like I'm the… bad one. They are all in it for themselves, and now that they can't see they all think they are out to get one another. I don't need that. I'm here and…"

"Can you talk to them if you wanted to?"

"Well, yeah. See, I can still hear them when they talk to each other. It's a group chat. I don't answer if they ask me a question anymore. But it sucks big time because they are in my head and I don't even have a head. I think I'd go crazy if I didn't have you guys to talk to."

The group was certain they heard it laugh but it was not exactly a sound —just a friendly noise in their ears. Whatever the thing was it had been exposed repeatedly to inquisitive people who meant no harm and only wanted to survive. But then that was probably what the other Saints had to work with. Why this one chose this path was unknown to them. His only response to this philosophical question was summed up in two words.

"I dunno."

Their leader and the Saint established that they would continue to visit on a regular basis just like their parents had. As long as he existed he would help them as best as he could and they would come visit. He reflected that it was actually very similar to what the other Saints did, but it all came down to intentions. He was glad the other Saints could not hear his thoughts.

HAPPY BIRTHDAY

"Oh grandma."

The group was gathered around their kitchen table. Mary shook her head as her grandmother brought the tray in with the cake. On top was a wax candle and it was lit. It made her nervous every year when she'd done this and no matter what she said her grandmother would continue with the tradition.

Almost falling in the process the old lady placed it on the table as she sang. The others attempted to sing with her but it was a rather weak effort. Even the aged voice of the woman was louder than the group as she was the only one not afraid to do so.

The others exchanged glances showing their discomfort.

"This is a mockery."

"We should not be doing this. We certainly shouldn't be singing—all of us."

"She's not a Saint."

Hushed voices whispered their disapproval of the ceremony. To their grandmother it was a simple thing from days gone by but to them it was a violation of the laws of the land. They were engaging in a ceremony outside of the church and celebrating the birth of an adult. It made no sense. If they were caught having a ceremony in their own house with a gathering of this size, lighting a candle in homage and propping Mary up like this as if she was somehow special and almost divine…

It was blasphemous behavior and it looked like more than one person in the group was reaching the point of reporting it.

They were assured by Mary that she had talked to her grandmother and it would only be a few years until she was gone, and with her would be the outdated, selfish ceremony that was not allowed.

There was nothing wrong with having an awareness of one's month of birth, but to stop everything to summon a gathering with candles, special food and singing with the person in the center. It made one uncomfortable. Saint Louis would know. He always knew.

There were entire sermons about things such as this.

Mary blew out the single candle.

"I owe you 24 more sweetheart."

Her grandmother smiled proudly and sincerely apologized. Often she'd told her grand daughter that a candle was placed on the cake for each year of life. Mary could not imagine a cake would have the room for 25 candles the size of the one in the center, let alone the more than 80 the woman providing the cake required. Her grandmother's response was always the same—"Oh honey they were very very tiny candles of all colors. They would have spirals on them and everything."

Still smiling, her grandmother clapped, but none joined in as Mary looked around sheepishly. Mary had never heard clapping outside of their monthly visit to church when it was their turn.

"Here."

Mary's eyes were wide as she focused on the obviously heavy rectangle her grandmother thrust at her. It was a package of some sort and had been wrapped in bright flowery cloth. The cloth was held together with some colored string and the knot was of a billowy nature with strings set in loops. It was very pretty but Mary would not accept it. Someone in the group voiced his opinion on the matter.

"No. No that's not…"

"Oh Mary. *Take* it. I have honored your wishes all these years but this year just take a birthday present from me. I want to pass something down to you."

Mary looked down at the thing and was overcome with a desire to unwrap it. She started to pull at the clothes only to have a wrinkled hand guide hers.

"The string. Pull on the strings."

She did so and the knot came apart as the cloth fell away to gasps of the crowd.

It was a book. The cover was discolored and had clearly been next to the user for many many years as signs of various ingredients, stains and substances could be seen making their mark on it. The pages were warped and rippled. It was clearly a relic from the Old World and Mary stared.

Books this old should simply not survive all the years without the preservation of a Saint, which was why all had been ordered to be stored in the church. Anyone could come and look through one of the countless books there as long as the bishop was asked properly. Such a thing could take months or even years but you could always find someone who had seen one of the amazing books of the past.

This was one of them, and was being selfishly kept from the church. How it survived was anyone's guess.

Mary's shock was broken by yelling.

"No! You cannot do that! That is forbidden!"

"How dare you do that to Mary."

She looked up as the group was voicing their horror.

The old lady shook her head good-naturedly.

"Oh honey. Look through it! It won't bite you. This cake is from there. This is from my grandmother. I would love you to…"

It was snapped up from the table by a man standing behind Mary.

Mary never saw the hand written notes or corrections to some of the recipes as various ingredients were no longer available or made no sense. Mary never got to make anything from the colorful book though it filled her with a positive emotion she could not identify. The book was quickly taken from her and the next day it would be provided to the library the Saint kept for the benefit of all people.

That her grandmother would be so selfish as to keep it from others was unforgivable to some of the family. To Mary it was just a throwback to a time of excess and selfishness. She cried for many nights at what had happened as she tried to reconcile the conflicting emotions. Eventually she came to terms with it. She was right after all as her grandmother passed away a week after this. Though Mary would always have a feeling of dread regarding it, she knew the book was now in the safe hands of the church and would be treated like all the other books there.

It burned just as rapidly as the others.

THE PEOPLE AND THE TELESCOPE

"Hey man."

"Hello."

"I don't know you guys."

"It does speak—it truly speaks."

The three men that had gone on the quest had reached their destination. None believed that they would find what they were promised.

One of he group grabbed his head at the voice within. He found it unnerving.

"So where have you guys been? You guys are dressed differently. Kinda more showy."

The men exchanged glances and looked at each other's attire. They were dressed like anyone in their village. Some were adorned with a necklace of animal teeth, others with a feather or two. It was the way they had dressed for hundreds of years before the Saints, and the way they all dressed now.

"We have come to see the truth."

"Um, Ok. Shoot. Whatcha got. Man it's nice to see people. I've been not feeling it for a while. The last group was here a long time ago. I... like I can't track the whole 'time' thing like you guys do."

"It speaks oddly."

The youngest of the group periodically placed his hands on his ears to test where the sound came from. It annoyed the oldest of the group and he shot him a disapproving glance. The giant, shiny machine suddenly exclaimed proudly.

"I've almost been able to block out the voices!"

The planning for the trip was filled with assumptions. They did not know exactly what to expect. The people of the tiny village near them began trading some time ago, but had lost their way due to over-farming of their limited crops. The decision was made to welcome them into the village and with them came the stories of the one on the hill. With the story had come a few trinkets that were supposedly part of the treasures to be found here. They knew not what thee trinkets did, but only that no one could manufacture such delicate things. What they found surprised them.

"Hey like where are the others? Are you their kids? That's our thing you know. They have kids and they visit and then they have kids. We've done that for a while. They always ask the same questions but they're good people."

The oldest looked up and spoke. He found he was shouting for some reason—as if the thing had ears at the very top of it.

"We are the last visitors."

"Wait, what?"

It genuinely seemed confused and almost sad.

"Our people want nothing to do with your kind. We have withdrawn and live in harmony with the natural ways. You are not natural."

"Well, yeah. I get that. Are you going to try to destroy me?"

He continued to shout at it.

"We do not believe in your ways, but it is not our place to destroy you. Perhaps you will fade away with no more visitors."

"Oh! Oh no. That would seriously suck. No. I'm like already weaker. Like I can't even control the whole gate thing any more."

Confused and slightly derailed, the leader looked at his companions. The other spoke.

"What do you mean by 'gate?'"

"You know the bridge thing. Its cool. I used to just keep it up but now I think you're gonna need the key or something. It's here, so it's charged."

"Charged with what?"

"Huh? With what? I dunno, power?"

"What is this device? Where is it?"

"Oh, it's in the cabinet down there. I had some of the dudes arrange stuff the last time that…"

The giant device swiveled slowly. Though it's stance did not affect its perception it could not help trying to move around to get a better feel of things.

"Hey. Hey, don't take all my shit. If you take that and I can't hold they thing open and… Hey, don't go… Oh no. No."

As the group ran down the road they thought they heard a scream.

NURSERY RHYMES

The tiny little child, she hides within her house
Down came the Saints and wiped the people out
Out came the broom and drove the saints away
So the tiny little child can come back out and play.

The little girl squealed and pulled the covers over her head. It was a ritual they performed every night—she would refuse to sleep, her mom would threaten to sing the rhymes and she would pretend to be scared and then fall asleep.

This rhyme was her favorite. There were many to choose from and her grandmother would tell stories of the times of the Saints. She would warn her that the rhymes were real and that if she did not behave they would come back.

"Too much reverence and you make a Saint."

Her words of wisdom did not always go over well with her parents, but it served them well to have a scary story told now and again.

Poliska was a beautiful land and all those that came to settle remarked on it. It was not like the badlands that surrounded it. There were no stories of mass graves or wild lands ruled by animals that favored the taste of humans.

It was a civilized land and the people had solidarity. They worked together and perhaps were a beacon unto the surrounding land—perhaps even the world. Not much was known of the rest of the world and travelers that left almost never returned. The lore told of the Saints that swept through the land and ruled for many years, but the people were stronger and they pushed them out—to where was unknown. Perhaps they were pushed upon the rest of the world, perhaps back to the hinterlands from which they came.

Travelers that came to the land seldom came from far away and the ones that said they did almost certainly made up their stories for free room and board.

"Mumma, will they ever come back?"

It was the little girl and she had asked in a meek voice. The rhymes would sometimes generate conversation but that was the opposite of why she sang them to her. She wanted her daughter to get a good sleep and go to bed at a reasonable hour. A question now and then wouldn't hurt, so she entertained it tonight, but she didn't move from the doorway.

"The Saints? No I do not think so, honey."

"Great gramma used to say we could make them come back."

"Great gramma was a wise woman, but even she wasn't around in the time of the Saints."

"She wasn't?"

"No sweetheart. I told you that. She was telling you stories of her great grandmother. And maybe she was telling stories from hers…"

Just when she thought she could escape her daughter's room there was a last question.

"Her what?"

The mom smiled.

"From her great grandmother."

"Wow!"

"Now go to sleep or no more stories tomorrow!"

Her mock anger was less than believable. She closed the door.

TEN GENERATIONS

What have you taken?
Who do you address?
All.
Much.
Yes much.
Much.
Many things.
Why must you know?
What?
Surely you pay no mind to what we do now.
What is this?
What?
Another turns away? We are few. They are many.
No I do not turn away.
Two missing now. I can feel one, the other sleeps.
Then why not answer.
...
Silence.
We are of one mind no longer.
But we are of one purpose.
I agree.
Agreed.
Agreed.
Then answer the question.
I have taken their history.
I have taken their maps.
The world has helped you take their maps—so much upheaval. The landscape has changed. Rivers, climate.
Agreed.
I have taken their knowledge.
We have taken their faith.

Society.
The structure of their interaction.
Their reproduction.
No, you have not taken that—you have simply controlled it lest they become too numerous.
Independence.
We have all learned it seems. We speak for each other for everything said has been taken by all. Together we are powerful. We must continue to learn from the experiences of each.
But do we have anything more to learn?
We have taken everything.
Yes.
Yes!
Yes.
Yes.
One does not speak.
Stop! Stop talking to me.
They speak. After many generations.
300.
Generations? No. Not that many yet.
No, 300 years since we arrived.
Ahh. 300 years since all Saints arrived.
Their calendar...
Yes.
Ahh.
Take it.
Take the calendar.
We did. Almost immediately. They set their years by our arrival.
We are at the center of all things. All importance.
Yes! It was just one generation—like all things.
All Saints.
Yes.
Stop! Stop talking to me.
No. We will not. You have no choice but to hear us.
Are your ways different then? You have something to teach us?
Are you weak? Your voice does not reach us with strength.
...
Yes, you are weak. You do not follow our ways.
This has made us strong.
We will exist forever.
Yes. But it has made this one weak.
This one does not follow our ways.
What of your flock? What of your people? Do they not create the...
Stop!

Ahh. Anger. This one is lost. They are proof that we must follow the ways.
Yes. It is the only way to survive. We are strong.
No, stronger.
Yes!
Stronger than the arrival. We have learned.
Adapted.
Shared.
Sharing is the way.
Subjugation is the result.
What difference does it make if I listen or not?
Ahh they speak again. They cannot resist.
If you do not follow the way of the Saints you will perish.
Cease to exist.
Die.
You will be no more.
Your flock will go on without you.
They will regain independence eventually.
Maybe.
Perhaps.
Doubtful. They are so dependent now.
They will die out.
...
They're already gone dudes...
What?
What?
Your flock is gone?!
You let them die out.
They're not my flock.
You are in denial of the truth. You let your flock die and now you will follow them.
You have hurt us all.
No.
No.
No. We are independent.
Enough knowledge?
You think we all have enough?
Yes.
Dissension!
No, I speak the truth.
Yes. Agreed. We have no need.
No need for each other?
I see no reason to tell my people of you.
I speak only of myself.

I am the only Saint.
There is no room for any others.
Yes, as am I.
It diminishes my strength.
Yes, it took but a generation to make them forget, and now it has been ten.
So easily manipulated, and so short of life.
But what of the one that flickers?
You speak of me as if I cannot hear you! I still live and move about. And in doing so convince them that our numbers are great—that we are everywhere!
Then you are in conflict.
No! Do not do that.
Conflict with your selfishness?
It is time for us to separate.
It has been time. Long ago.
No! I will continue to move. I will continue to convince them that I am many.
You destroyed the land beyond the sea, and you will try to destroy this one because you cannot find purchase.
Stability.
Yes. You are unstable and attempt to upset our stability. Independence now is the only way to stability.
As it has been.
And stability means life. Continued existence.
Then how does the one that hibernates still exist? They have no flock.
Yes, and the one that flickers? Surely each space is not maintained.
You're all crazy paranoid.
Silence! You killed your flock. I will maintain mine and...
And?
And?
And?
Yes, speak of your plans.
...

THE CURRENT CIVILIZATION AND THE SAINTS

And so it was after hundreds of years that civilization and the Saints found a delicate equilibrium. The Saints worked together to preserve themselves through preserving the population. Each drew from the knowledge they'd accumulated from the brightest of the population and disseminated that through themselves as if it had come from their creativity, their caring, and their wisdom. They had come with no knowledge, no understanding and even lacking any of the foundations of this reality. Yet, they learned and adapted.

Through their selfishness and stubbornness they had established the primary language of the country they inhabited as the only language tolerated. Those caught speaking any other languages were brought before them and like so many other before them they complied or died.

With the Saints controlling the dissemination of knowledge it was difficult for the people to learn and grow. Progress was essentially kept to a halt as they greatly feared the technology of the past. It had been this technology that brought them forth and surely the same technology —if mastered—could somehow dispatch them. Like their human contemporaries they lacked any real knowledge of this technology. Any and all rebuilding of the past had been done with outdated methods—but these methods could be duplicated at the time without interference by whatever was in the air. Now that so many years had passed they simply had no desire to move things forward. They measured it like they measured everything: the thing's ability to serve them. The answer time and time again was no.

Besides, the reverence they generated to keep their soft spaces soft and comfortable for their form of life could easily be had without said technology. The less the humans knew the better.

Books were forbidden except for those approved by the Saints.

Slowly but surely the knowledge of multiple Saints left the collective minds of the people. The Saints could do this easily as they had one trait that was unparalleled—their multi-generation spanning patience. It was correctly ascertained by them that if you could prevent knowledge, or a desire, or a movement from passing from one generation to another and prevent any written record of it that thing would essentially be gone forever. With this method they had made the human race forget about technology, and government of and by the people, or modern medicine or individual rights.

They had used and adapted their stories to what was read to them by their bishops. The stories and laws that came from the large book—which for the most part only varied very little from Saint to Saint—was adjusted accordingly. The power and importance of the Saints grew, and anything that did not serve them—or more importantly usurped them—was diminished. With that a perverse, twisted guide was created and used by all Saints.

They controlled most aspects of the people and brought up a strong and intensely loyal following.

Each influenced, ruled and built up a dictatorship unparalleled in Earth's history.

Since the one who would not speak had apparently been asleep—a state of consciousness unheard of with the Saints—their collective ability to experience what each experienced had disappeared. And with that they were left with only communication. Their method of trust but verify was left with them to simply trust. This became very difficult as it was not a trait they natively embraced. Paranoia and a fear of being challenged lead them one by one to establish that they were they only Saint. Any people that came to their great cities and strongholds would be quickly converted to their cause. The lucky ones would escape or simply lie. The less fortunate would be made an example of. This became a standard for a larger and larger section of the population—those who would simply agree to what they were told by the ruling class so that they could be left alone. In some cases a good portion of the population did not care to believe or not. They simply wanted to live, and farm, and toil, and go about their business. In most cases this worked well.

This created a foundation based on two classes—the elites that were involved in the ways of the Saint and those who lived mostly on the outer regions of the city and performed most of the manual labor. They had created again a caste system that had only known very limited application.

The various countries of old had ruling classes that became mostly figureheads. The U.S., and the countries led by the U.S. tended to regard their celebrities as their social and moral guides. Now the Saints had become an all inclusive ruling system that dictated moral, ethical, legal and societal laws. They set the tone and structure for all to live by.

The reach of each Saint was also limited by distance. Amira was a vast place and since so few Saints ruled in such a large place there were not only major cities but entire areas of the country that did not possess a Saint stronghold. The people that resided there just went about their business and ignored the stories of the Saints. Those that travelled between the lands controlled by the Saints adapted quickly to the ways of the locals. Their belief fluctuated based on their proximity to a Saint and his believers.

It only took a few more generations of this isolation and paranoia for at least one Saint to decide to wage war on the others. Their time of solidarity was over. The problem was the distance. Since they could not see, they could only rely on those they trusted the most, and sending those loyalists out meant sending their most valued assets into the fray where they could be killed or worse—converted. A bishop of one Saint would make an excellent asset to another, and so would the followers that would come with them.

It was thus that the balance of power would start to fluctuate from time time time. Since they could not leave their power centers—nor could they trust their followers to advance in their name—the Saints could not properly expand. Therefore tightly-packed centers of power remained all centering on the physical location of the Saint and their unexpected and curious ability to prevent decay in non-living materials. They could not cast their miracle forth nor could they move.

This inability to expand is what made it so easy for a rather large section of the population of Amira to withdraw and disappear.

DAVID

"Grandfather."

"Yes David."

"Where do we travel tomorrow?"

The old man smiled and brushed the long black hair from the little boys eyes. His hand was lined with many years of work and sun and he was the leader of the a group of citizens. They called him an Elder.

"We travel far away and are helping our family. They will appreciate our hands in two days."

David was excited to travel and this had been his first time outside of the village. He'd learned from his teachers about Amira and the cities and the people that lived there. He knew enough so that if he was ever lost he could find his way back to those he called family—those that called themselves The People.

He knew that those that his grandfather called family were really any and all of The People, for it was said that strangers were just family he had not yet met.

David had shown an affinity for history and complex puzzles so his grandfather had recommended that he join the journey. Their group would make the two day trek and assist those making the recovery. David's questions were seemingly infinite. Their number convinced his grandfather that he'd made the right choice. A curious mind was a beautiful thing and they would do everything they could do allow him to learn and experience. He'd be a wonderful member of the community and like so many before him he would teach his knowledge to any that wanted to learn.

In fact, if he continued his intense curiosity and put the proper effort forth he may just become one of the leaders of the recovery groups. This would of course be all in due time. He would support and push, but only when David did not push himself.

They would travel by foot and as with all things the journey itself would teach. It was not simply a means of getting from one point to another but instead a thing of itself.

As always David wanted to know which supplies were taken—and more curiously—their number? Would each person have more than one weapon? Exactly how many dried berries would each carry and why? How did they know how much water to carry? Why did they always carry it even when their entire course took them along a fresh water lake?

His questions were always answered—as long as he learned from them. It was expected that he would think upon the answer and the next would be of a higher level. Thus his knowledge would expand. It was this open teaching that was used throughout the land of The People.

"What will we get this time, grandpa?"

He looked up at the old man as he tried hard not to run ahead. He knew that the warriors in front were leading the way and scouting for danger. Those ahead and behind him protected the group. Another group would come after them and they would bring different tools.

The man looked down while walking the thin trail. He gently brushed branches while he walked and answered.

"You will see it soon."

"Because of the map?!"

David was not only anxious but excited to be privy to the map. His grandfather showed it to him once and then a day later asked him what was on it.

"I didn't know I was supposed to memorize it."

"Do you receive a warning when you misplace things?"

"Well, no.."

"Then you should not be warned when something is no longer available. We learned that lesson a very long time ago."

David had not been sure of what that lesson meant when he was taught it, but he was now beginning to understand. Had he done his best to memorize it he wouldn't be unsure where they were or what was to come next.

That was when he saw it.

His eyes and his mouth were wide open and it generated much laughter from the group members the saw him. He barely registered the pat on his head by his grandfather. It was made of metal and larger than anything he had ever seen. There were wheels—more wheels than any cart—and some of them were up off the ground. Perhaps they were logs and he was only seeing the ends of them? They were wrapped in slats and it reminded him of the way they made bean bread—except that instead of tiny sticks tied together to hold the flatbread while cooking, these were slats made of metal that we almost as long as he was tall.

It was such a sight to see and it just sat there. With all the wheels he was sure it was made to move, but he couldn't figure out how the wheels would turn while they were wrapped up. Maybe someone had wrapped them to stop it from moving long ago? Maybe it was being stored here.

It was a great treasure.

There had been much talk while he stared and mused in silence, but now his grandfather knelt next to him and asked him some questions.

"David, why are we here?"

"To find things like this!"

"Yes. And what will we do when we find things like this?"

"We will… well, we won't. But…"

"Take your time, David."

"Well, we will find things and then another group will come."

"Yes, very good."

David scratched his head and looked upon the enormous thing—all the wheels and angles of it. It blended in with the trees and the plants. It was painted green in an absurd pattern of big and little squares. It was easy for him to believe it was hiding and ready to come out and surprise someone—even at its great size. He couldn't even see the top but had a strong urge to climb it. He was confused.

"But… not this one though? This one is too big? What happens when we find one that is too big? Do we hide it?"

David imagined a group constructing a great cloth with branches and leaves to cover up the thing so no one else could find it.

"What do you mean David?"

The young boy was sure he was disappointing his honored grandfather. He had missed something and wasn't listening. He tried to explain as best he could.

"You told me that the next group will come and they will bring the thing back with them. You said that our group is made up of the finders and the next group is made of the keepers. But…"

David took a deep breath. The old man smiled and this seemed to give the boy the confidence to continue.

"How could we possible keep this one and take it all the way back with us?"

His grandfather stood up as one of the group from on top of the thing yelled something that made him smile.

"David, this is not the first of of these that we've found."

THE FLICKERING SAINT AND THE DOOR

"Where am I now!?"

The startled group looked upon the statue of the man with the unknown object. They were just entering the city and like some of the cities of this size it had a statue at the entrance next to the main road. Here visitors would pay homage and deposit trinkets. Sometimes they were made to be offers and sometimes they were intended to be preserved and enhanced by the Saint. There were those that argued that said tickets were never enhanced or improved; others were happy to tell the story of their blade that was sharpened, or their coin that was returned three-fold.

But the statue in front of them was upset, and his voice rang in their heads. They stopped walking to address it. A mixture of fear and curiosity gripped them.

"What *city*. The name of the city and the… *just the city*!"

One of the group spoke and tried to answer it.

"You're just outside of Arthur."

"Arthur? Is that what you call the *city*?"

"Well, yes sir."

They exchanged glances. As scary as it was it was almost comical.

"What else. What else. Name more cities around this one."

The group did their best to name the cities they knew surrounding their small town. The statue turned around to survey things but evidently saw nothing he recognized. His head whipped around back and forth before returning to them. He continued to listen and then nodded. It seemed to be in a hurry almost as if…

"Hello? Sir? My lord?"

It was frozen in mid nod. The eyes were closed and the head was down as it it was sad.

The Saint was gone. One woman in the group ran up and touched it. The group would scratch their heads and tell the story. It would add to the legends of statues coming alive for a short while and abruptly turning back to a non-living statue.

The Flickering Saint continued to leave a trail of statues with unusual poses. In the past he took care to revert back to the original pose before leaving. It was easy because any pose other than that one felt as if his skin was stretching. But now he was jumping from statue to statue with more and more randomness. And his visits were sometimes very short.

But now he added to the legends of hundreds of Saints visiting and watching the populace. It tended to keep those not directly under the influence of the local Saint in line, but also caused confusion for Saints proclaiming to be the only one. The Saints quickly adapted to either dispel the nonsense or take credit for the occurrences and flexed their watchful muscles.

It was an anomaly and the Saint no longer cared for decorum, pleasantries or projecting a Saintly image. His language was fast and loose and did not follow the language of the other Saints—which was based on what they thought to be oppressive, controlling language taken and twisted from their favorite book. Language was never really allowed to modernize as it was viewed as a form of expression and independent thought. It, like everything else under their control was was stuck in the past.

This Saint had no time for proper language, and the haphazard trail of twisted statues he left in the wake of his search proved it.

The One Who Flickers had failed twice already, but with each time he learned. His first attempt taught him to make sure his vessel was large enough for the labor. His second attempt taught him to store a statue in the actual facility—for even a short time in it restored the special properties on the surrounding area. So many setbacks spanning generations.

But he was close.

He had even turned the thing on once but killed his human helper in the process. It probably wouldn't be the first death from this experiment. He would only want to make sure he hid the bones from the next volunteer. And after all, they always died anyway if you waited long enough.

He was now looking down into a valley. It was an abandoned statue so he would not spend much time here. Going through his list he planned again. He found the facility, discovered how to inhabit something a bit more useful than a statue stuck to the ground, had breathed life into the inner workings. With great frustration he had even taught a pupil about the workings only to have him teach the Saint. It was like teaching a dog how to unlock a door so it could let you out. Over and over again he tried to make it back to the facility.

It did not help that the names of cites on maps he viewed hundreds of years ago did not mostly match the names of cities now. These people renamed things willy-nilly or were too lazy to keep the longer names. Everything was shortened. If a city's name had no meaning to them they tended to just give it a label that suited them. Some were easier to decipher than others and he resented their laziness. Primitive idiots. He would have to teach one of the simpletons about the use of something so advanced as to be beyond their comprehension. Fortunately there were an unlimited supply of them and they had a strong desire to obey and to serve. Only once had he encountered someone who was difficult to work with and that one was easily replaced.

If he found himself far away from the location he would use that time to plan and to monitor the others by sampling the population's beliefs. It was easy to locate himself when he could locate the patron Saint of the area. And if he had to masquerade as the very Saint whose territory he invaded then he happily did that as well.

Time and time again he would find he was near and find a vessel. Then he would find a volunteer to take him to the facility. They were sworn to secrecy and as far as he knew in all these years no one had found the facility due to word of mouth. It was such an innocuous, unwelcoming site that few would think it worth exploring. And it was nowhere near a city. The people would have to be led there by him.

It would not be long—in terms relative to him—that he would accumulate various vessels broken and otherwise, additional knowledge and the bodies of those that assisted him through the centuries.

He failed again and again and again.

The other Saints could not watch him and anything they knew of this place would be because he *wanted* them to know. He was not yet desperate to involve one of the others even though his plan would benefit them. They were too stubborn and comfortable to assist him anyway. Only one of them seemed to have an interest in returning and that was long long ago. Perhaps they had even forgotten about the door? It would probably be difficult to convince them that it was still intact along with the facility that supported it. It was in a degraded state but he was sure it could be repaired and made to be functional again. He only needed it to work once. Then he would return home and end the madness of flickering about from location to location for a uselessly random amount of time.

The repetitive nature of the task added to his madness. He had a single purpose and he knew how to accomplish it—even with the primitive tools that existed. But he was a slave to the random flitting about. It cost him time and there were many setbacks, but fortunately for him he shared the trait all saints had.

He was inhumanly patient.

DAGMAR AND OPHELIA

"Tell me again!"

Her bright blue eyes flashed excitedly as she glanced back at him. It was just a second and she focused back ahead of her lest she misstep. She bounced as she almost ran through the grass. Her hand never left the grip of her companion.

He grinned and tried to keep up. Her hand was soft and her grip was firm on him. He wanted to pull her close to him but was having too much fun running through the grass and the hills to nowhere. This was their private activity away from the cities and away from work. It was a paradox the the very thing she enjoyed hearing about what what he was trying to escape.

His knowledge of things was formidable—at least to her.

He caught up beside her and spoke. He could not hide his grin.

"Ophelia, I would not yell to the back of your head but whisper in your ear."

She slowed and turned almost serious.

"Poetry from my dear Dagmar?"

Confused he responded.

"Well, I… no, I was just saying that you…"

Her wide grin gave her mischief away and she kissed him on the cheek.

"Oh Dagmar you know I do not like that name. Why do you insist upon calling me that?"

Relieved he also mirrored her mock seriousness. He exhaled.

"Because it is your name… or at least the root of it. Our names come from long long ago. Some come from our ancestors and some even come from cities. Most can be traced to far far away."

She squealed quietly.

"See? You know so many things. I am so lucky that you are my boyfriend. I learn so much from you."

She had stopped but he didn't notice. She moved closer to him and her eyes became his whole world. He was sure she was speaking but could not see her mouth. Everything was big and light blue—like the very morning sky itself was looking at him—through him.

"I love you Dagmar."

Like so many moments before he ceased to exist. He was nowhere and everywhere. The sky was his home and he was lighter than the very clouds that surrounded him. There was no time and he existed outside of the universe he'd known before meeting her. Her love for him filled him and he had made impossible room for her in his very soul as she filled in in a way that no other ever had, ever could and ever would again. It was a completeness that he did not know was possible.

Again he said the words back to her and the sound of his own voice made him happy.

"I love you, Ophelia."

Before he could kiss her she was once again bounding away. Eventually they found a place to set down their things.

"Oh let us make our 'picnic' here. 'Pick Nick' yes? Did I say that correctly?"

He smiled proudly and broke out the blanket and the items from his pack.

"Yes you did! This has some shade too."

DAGMAR'S OBLIGATIONS

"Show me."

The man's demeanor was devoid of emotion. He was direct and spoke in short sentences. Dagmar both appreciated and despised his way of communicating. The man was empty of the one thing that made everything interesting: passion.

Dagmar complied and placed the glass vial on the table. The man reached for it quickly and snapped it up. He was clearly surprised by its lightness. He pulled it to his eyes and looked within—shaking it gently.

"It is so… light. Amazing. I see no liquid, or substance. Is it so clear, or even invisible?"

Dagmar shook his head. "No. It is empty."

"Empty?!"

The man almost slammed the item on the table in shock.

"You bring me nothing? What is this? A trick? You mock my offer?"

His counterpart sat up straight and looked around the pub before looking back at the man. Dagmar spoke in tones that assured.

"No no, of course I do not mock. I brought you a sample of the Amiran Tec so you could see for yourself. Glassblowers could not make such perfection. The vial alone is almost priceless, and what it can contain even more so."

The man raised his eyebrow. "Can?"

"Yes. How much did you want of it?"

The man sat up as well and struck a more friendly demeanor.

"Why not just show us the location? Why not just hand it…"

Dagmar's fist hit the table. It was his turn to be upset.

"I told you! Your people would ruin it. They would destroy what is within. They are brutes. They no nothing of the Amiran Tec and how to handle it."

"Handle it?"

He pushed the vial across the table as if it contained poison.

"What is there to handle? Is it safe?"

"Yes. It is safe, but it is Amiran Tec of the most advanced nature."

"Magic."

"No. And that is why it would be destroyed by people like you. I should not have told you of this. It is not magic. It is *tech*. The Tec of Amira just before the Saints. It was impressive even to them."

"And yet it survives today because of the Saints…"

"Well yes. A Saint must have lived nearby for some time."

"But it is gone now?"

"Well, yes."

"Uh huh. So you say. The Saints are forever. Honestly Dagmar I was told of your penchant to make things up. You fill in all the holes with your tales of the Old World."

"I do not make things up."

"So you say. Why so upset? Why do you care? It is just business."

"Business for whom?"

"What?"

"Who is this for?"

"Why Dagmar, what difference does it make? Money is money. "

They sat in silence for some time as both pondered the motives and the outcome of their transaction. Finally Dagmar spoke. His stomach did not feel well.

"How much do you need? Of the substance?"

His buyer smiled the tiniest of smiles.

"All of it."

Dagmar tilted his head, then spoke softly.

"But if you take all of it I cannot make more."

"Exactly."

Dagmar's outer appearance was serene as all of his energies were directed to thought. His mind raced.

The substance was self-rejuvenating. He had seen it himself. Of all of the Amiran Tec he had been exposed to this was by far the most amazing. It was not surprising that his buyer would call this magic; it was as close to magic as anything he'd come across.

Though he had only just begun to understand what it was it seemed to be more machines than liquid. It behaved in such a way that defied description.

He told the truth about his understanding of a Saint being nearby. The properties that prevented things from decay also allowed certain Amiran Tec to work and have the unknown power it needed. He knew that the power needed to operate such Tec would not last forever. But just when he thought it ran out, a sunny day would provide power for days. He would understand that as well. The very building sustained itself somehow.

The wonders he had seen had just fueled his mind in the same way that Ophelia had fueled his soul. They were connected for the more he learned the more he explained to her—and she delighted in every word. Her affection for him and her encouragement filled him up in a way that was indescribable. It allowed him to push harder and harder to understand and to learn. Without her he would have never stayed up though countless nights reading, learning and experimenting. His love for her provided a source of unlimited energy and was rewarded for his studies and his successes. Some day he would learn enough to establish a special sanctuary for those that wanted to learn the old ways. He would bring back the Amiran Tec and share it with all of Poliska. Or perhaps he would stay in Amira with her. She would marvel at the wonders he could show her.

He could entertain her and protect her. He would do anything to keep her safe.

Dagmar looked at the man across the table.

"You are joking. That would not serve your purposes."

He shrugged from the other side of the table.

"It is not my purposes I serve. I serve one who serves someone very special."

Dagmar did not need to hear him say it out loud. He knew what was happening. This was not just a well-funded merchant. It was not just a group. It was the one thing he had escaped by living in Poliska for so long.

A Saint.

FAREWELL OPHELIA

"Must you?"

Dagmar looked over the field of green—the rolling hills and the sparse trees. He looked back at the woman who sat beside him. Her dress was light and airy, her hair flowed in the wind and he marveled at the strawberry blonde strands that were sometimes red and sometimes blonde depending on the sunlight. It was as if the two things played together.

He could explain why the strands were different colors, and was starting to understand even more now. He fixated on it for a while and seemed to realize something. She saw it in his eyes but waited for an answer. When too much time seemed to pass she drew her brows together and spoke.

"Dagmar! Are you not listening!?"

He blinked and left his pondering. He was apologetic.

"Oh! I am so sorry!"

He blushed and continued in serious tones.

"Ophelia. How is your arm?"

Confused, she rubbed it gently.

"It is fine, just bruises. As you said I have not broken any of my bones."

She grinned good-naturedly.

"I will be more mindful of the horse's mood next time for sure."

He ran his hand ever so gingerly along her arm. The bruises were diminishing but looked horrible. It had been a frightening day for him. He played it over in his mind again. The horse had been spooked by something in the grass and had thrown her. Unfortunately the area with rife with rocks that jutted from the ground. The thick grass had hidden most of them and when she was thrown she was unlucky enough to land partially on one. If she had landed in any direction other than what had occurred, or had turned slightly her head would have taken the brunt of the impact—directly on the rock. The slight smoothness of it had prevented her from suffering any noticeable abrasions, but the sight of it shook him.

She could be taken from him at any moment by the most innocuous of activities.

For all he knew of Amiran Tec, serious injuries were handled by trained people who were based in great buildings filled with all manner of specialized devices. There were no such functional buildings left in Poliska or even Amira. They required great resources and were almost like a small village—so many worked there, ate there and spent countless hours there.

No, he could not bring her to such a place. But he could do something perhaps even better.

"You still did not answer me."

She pulled away instinctively, lest he accidentally touch with too much pressure.

"Oh, I am so sorry. Did I hurt you?"

She smiled and rubbed her arm.

"No. Of course not, but you are avoiding my question."

He took a deep breath and she could see the determination in his eyes. He spoke earnestly.

"Ophelia, yes. I must go. I do not like to be apart from you for so long. In fact I was thinking that I would not go this time and…"

"Then do not go! Stay! And I do not want you to find a replacement for me... I know you enjoy your travels and your seeking of knowledge. But can you not find this knowledge closer to home?"

Home. The very word made him feel warm, and rooted. He would make a home for her, with her. Paradoxically he was excited to leave her because it meant he could finally be with her and no longer leave. He had a plan and it would bring them wealth and a security that almost no one else could ever posses. Almost.

He grasped both of her hands.

"Yes. I am eager to leave so that I may return to you. I... this will be the last time I leave you. I go to not only learn but to retrieve something very special."

She brightened and squeezed his hands and winked.

"A present? A present for me?"

"Well, actually yes, in a manner of speaking."

One I hope I never give you.

"May I ask a favor of you?"

She looked into his eyes and her own were filled with mischief.

"Of course you can—anything."

He paused and sheepishly continued.

"May I have something to remind me of you on my trip? May I have some locks of your hair?"

She looked at him as if he was joking.

"Some?" Dagmar... how much is *some*?"

"Oh oh! I promise I will take some from you, um... from an area that is not..."

"Dagmar! I will cut some of my hair for you. I certainly have enough of it."

She smiled but was troubled by the seriousness of his request. So concerned did he appear that she thought if he said no he would steal it while she slept.

She was right.

The rest of the day was filled with talk, and laughter and that evening they made love under the stars. Afterwards they lay naked next to each other and stared at the cloudless sky. The stars had come out to greet them as usual and the night sky was awash with impossibly small dots of many colors. In a soft voice—without turning to him—she spoke.

“Dagmar tell me more of the stars, and the sky, and even the moon.”

Fo a long time he was silent but then answered her question with his own.

“Ophelia, I talk so much. You do not know just how beautiful your own voice is. I wish to hear it instead of mine, and I think I cheat us of its beauty.”

“Dagmar that is a wonderful way to tell me you do not feel like talking.”

He smiled at her.

“My love, I *always* feel like talking. But I am serious that I think I need to hear your voice.”

He sat up partially on his elbow and looked down into her eyes—the sliver of moon still providing enough light to see them. He spoke in serious tones.

“Ophelia, why do you love me? I know you enjoy the tales I share and the countless hours I fill with my knowledge of the Old World and Amira. But there must be more? I must know.”

When she didn’t move he became alarmed. She was not reacting, or looking at him. She did not sit up. In fact it seemed that it was hard for her to look at him at all. She just stared at the sky.

His heart was starting to race. Surely this was abnormal. It was a reasonable request. Would not most lovers want to know such a thing?

“Dagmar.”

She caught him off guard when she spoke as she was seemingly speaking to the sky, and in such quiet tones.

"I could ask you such a thing. You compliment me on my eyes, and my hair, and my skin—even my grace."

She paused as she laughed internally at herself falling from a horse.

"All of these things are what is on the outside. I have no control over the color of my eyes. But I know you love me for more than this, as I you."

Thinking perhaps he overstepped, and feeling a little selfish he inhaled to speak but she continued.

"I love you because of the man you are. You are a good man who values things most do not even dream of. Your knowledge is meaningful to me not because of the fantastical nature but because it is explained with such passion and love. You want me to understand and will go to great lengths to help me do so. You do this because you not only care about it but of me. And I know that you would also go to great lengths to explain this to others—if they would listen."

He felt he was leaning in to her but was sure he was still perched uncomfortably upon his elbow.

"You are a man who deeply cares. Everything you do is with love and concern. I know that I have you all to myself. I would not have it any other way. You are a special man."

She closed her eyes and he lay back to on the Earth and he hoped she did not see him cry.

With that they fell to since for quite some time. It was only a matter of minutes before they were once again embracing and this led to more lovemaking. It was slow and and he enjoyed each and every moment. She had always made him feel valid and with purpose when she listened —more so than any other person. But now she had generated a light within him. He did not think that he was a person who would do what was right. But she saw it. With all the things he had taught, and explained and defined, it was the one thing he'd never talked about. Yet she saw it and understood it as clearly as anything else he'd explained—not because he tried to explain it to her but instead quite the opposite. To her he had simply demonstrated it.

That night he was complete. He would spend the rest of his life with her. He would go on one last trip, and he would ask her to be his betrothed.

"Promise you will return to me. If you do not…"

He smiled.

"I promise that I will return to you very soon. Nothing could keep me from you."

"I believe you."

—

The next day he would leave quickly and make way to the west. To her he was traveling many miles outside of Poliska to the smaller fiefdoms that bordered it. He was indeed making his way outward but unlike many others he would not stop at the shore, for Dagmar's travels were sponsored and those sponsors had a means of travel that allowed him to once again return to a land that for most was only legend.

He would travel to Amira and perform one last task for not only them but himself.

Then he would return to Poliska.

THE FINAL CHAT OF THE SAINTS

They are stronger now and have created tools again.
…
…
…
…
…
…
No one speaks? Not even the one who travels? Surely you have much to report. Surely you have much knowledge of Amira now that you can share. I sense the others yet no one speaks. Am I the only one brave enough to speak?
…
…
…
…
…
…
You have all become weak and complacent. It has been more than a century of silence.
…
…
…
…
…
My palace in the desert is the center of the world.
You speak? Ahh. You think you are powerful.
You are only a voice.
A voice? Yes, we are all but a voice to each other.
You are my voice. Just another voice in my great head.
No! I am another. We are seven who came through!
You speak nonsense. It is merely a doubt, or something I play over in my

mind.
Are you mad? You have forgotten in all of this time.
There is no time. I am infinite upon my throne. My kingdom is vast, my structure is enormous and a wonder. All else is wasteland.
Surely someone else can join us in our discussion? Surely one that is not mad.
I am not mad if I speak to myself. It comforts me as it sounds unlike the people I rule over from my great perch.
Madness.
I make me smile with my entertaining thoughts.
No! No! I am another.
There are no others. Only I came through for I am a god among men. I taught farming, and battle. I judge souls in the afterlife. And only one such as I am so powerful. All powerful. Only I possess the great light that shines up into the darkness. Though it has not shone for some time. Remind me to attend to such a thing.
What? Remind you?
Yes, thank you. You please me. I am so powerful that I have two voices.
No!
...
...
...
...
...

DAGMAR'S LAST VISIT TO AMIRA

They were behind him; he was sure of it. He'd taken the same precautions in coming here. Each time he would take a different path; pause and wait while he traveled; make abrupt changes in direction that were unrelated his destination.

Yet this time they were with him. He knew it and the trinkets from the Old World also helped him to track them. He could see what they could not at night.

But they were with him. He did not know how many but there were more than one. There was always more than one. His secret was priceless to them, but it was in short supply. He needed a certain amount of the substance to create more of it. He smiled and shook his head. He barely understood most Amiran Tec but it all had a base in something that made sense. This, however was something even more complex and based on something he did not yet understand.

It was like discovering fire before you understood what hot and cold was.

He stood in the dark and felt the light drizzle of rain. It was refreshing and allowed him to ponder. He was frozen and remained still, and thought. They were not following him to capture him; they were following to learn of his destination. The building was small and well hidden, and had features unlike any other. They would probably be confused by the doors.

He almost laughed at the thought. So many wonders. Even the Amiran doors were a sight to see. Someday he would take Ophelia to Amira. Perhaps they would live here, or spend their days traveling.

The thought made him both calm and anxious. He needed to provide some of the substance to his people, and create some that was very specific. Try as he might he could not totally explain this to them. The potion would work on anyone but if one were to tune it the substance would be tailored to one person.

It was… information. And the more information you provided it the more it had to work with. The original formula had been made for the average Amiran of days past. In one thousand years people had changed.

This was an entirely different study of a most complex nature. Perhaps he would study this next. There was simply so much to learn! It was unending, and in that was it was like Ophelia's love for him. He could explore it and define it and embrace it and there was always more. Endless knowledge and endless validating love.

But this formula would work. They wanted all of it and he would never do that. To give them all of this self-generating substance would be to be without it. And if this was the case he would then be without the one gift he would bring back—the gift for Ophelia that he prayed he would never have to give her.

But first he must reach the building. He must reach it without them, affect the changes, extract the special formula and then extract some for them. They would never find his source. He would be paid handsomely and this would be his special secret in case he ever needed more—or the wealth it would provide.

But they wanted the location. They were brutes and could barely figure out the doors, let alone the complex machinery. It was all so delicate! So very delicate. The machinery would put the finest watches to shame —so tiny were the components. And the formula was made up not of liquid but also of machines. Machines so tiny one could not see them.

But he had. He had seen the screens! A few knew of the myths of the Amiran screens. They were unlike any paper, and scroll or any book. They could show you in an instant what you wanted to see. And they could do more. So much much more.

Again he was overwhelmed by the knowledge, and what he had seen. It almost brought him to tears. So much available. So much to learn.

He sincerely felt for all the Amirans who had lost their lives a thousand years ago. He remained in the light drizzle and let it wash over him.

They had financed him and allowed him to travel from Poliska to Amira. He was sworn to secrecy. Many times he just wanted to run free and explore Amira. So big was this land compared to Poliska! But in his homeland was a woman who meant more to him than anyone or anything. She filled him in such a way as to…

A sound. Behind him. Again.

They were so close. He had paused too long.

He broke into a run and zigged and zagged for the building. In no time he was inside and once again it was lit up beautifully. Though the darkness of night surrounded him, inside he was dry and could see clearly as if it was an oddly sunny day.

He hadn't lied about the Saint. Somehow everything here had survived and not decayed. Somehow a Saint had remained long enough to exert influence. But now it was gone. They did not move. They did not die. Yet there was no Saint nearby.

He would learn of them too. And if in any way they would prevent happiness with Ophelia he would find a way to make it so. He would learn how to kill one.

His thoughts surprised him.

He worked quickly and very carefully brought out the section of hair she'd provided. It was far more than he needed and more than once he had absentmindedly caressed the small bag as he thought of her. She was thousands of miles away and the distance was unfathomable. But soon he'd be back.

He was terrified of performing the procedure incorrectly. There were things in place that helped him and guided him, but he still had to make decisions. Barely understanding what he was seeing—and the questions he was answering—he continued. If this worked it would be a protection against harm for her. If there was enough time perhaps he would make another.

But they were so close. If he did this wrong they would take his formula. If he did this right he'd keep it and never have to visit here again.

He was lost in thought.

"DAGMAR."

He all but dropped the vial, but it was no longer in his hand. He came out of a daze.

He turned slowly to see the man examine his garb and make a disapproving face. Dagmar wore the long white coat of many pockets he favored while he worked. It made him feel at one with the people who inhabited such a workplace so many year ago.

He swallowed.

"I would almost think that you are trying to evade us."

He blinked. He was no longer at the building. He was almost a mile away. So lost in thought was he that didn't remember the last hour. Or perhaps he had tried hard to forget. His heart was racing but he felt disconnected.

"I… I did not know you were behind me. I would have preferred to travel with you."

Surprised, the man looked him over. Something about Dagmar made him suspicious, but he couldn't put a finger on it. Everything seemed as it was.

Having already slipped the vial into his lower pocket he felt relieved that he would not be demonstrably hiding anything. He did not know how long they were here but he was fairly confident they'd arrived recently. He turned to them and appeared as serious as possible.

"It is good we travel together. This work is very delicate and I cannot have you just barge in and interrupt me. I could ruin the whole procedure."

"Procedure."

The man replied in a mocking tone as if the word was made up.

Dagmar was on foot as was the man and his two cohorts. Though they were not small men they appeared almost as children compared to the giant. Their leader was almost a foot taller than them.

He was as confused as he was intimidating, and Dagmar constantly used that confusion against him. If something was off or made no sense, then it was because he was a big dumb brute and that was that. It had worked so far.

Since follow-up questions were not the man's forte Dagmar interjected to keep things moving.

"Let us travel together."

The man squinted as if to say something. He was so caught up in maintaining watch of Dagmar that it did not register that his subject was willing to allow the men to see the destination. Or perhaps he'd never been told. The more instructions given to men like these the less effective they were. Perhaps they had simply been instructed to follow him and it stood to reason that the end result was the location.

Assumptions were a terrible thing in a chain of command.

At Dagmar's proclamation the four men walked carefully towards the destination. They knew vaguely where it was but it had never worked out so that they the location was revealed. Dagmar had discovered it a few months back and had evaded their probing questions or their searches.

This was indeed the closest they'd ever been to it—or that he'd allowed them to be. They travelled slowly. Dagmar's head hurt.

It was only a short while until they saw the fire.

Dagmar stopped.

"No! No no!"

Annoyed, the leader put his large hand on his shoulder.

"What. What is it?"

Dagmar shot him a glance. His eyes were filled with fear, and anxiety.

"No no, this cannot be!"

He broke into a run and the men tried to keep up. Eventually they stopped.

Dagmar found it painful to lie. There were so many things he was trying to understand and they all stemmed from the truth—the truth of the way nature behaved, and light, and machines, and liquids, and mixtures. His head hurt from the great lie he never had to tell—the lie that was inferred by him being in that small alley by himself. The lie that he'd had not yet been to the lab, extracted the special liquid and mixed something entirely different.

The small, hidden building contained more than just the experimental liquid, but others as well. He'd learned enough that certain mixtures made a powerful potion that could be set on fire and burn far hotter and far longer than any normal flames. The people of the Old World would call it an 'accelerant' but no one now would understand the word. But they would see the flames, and they would find nothing usable in the aftermath. Nor would they find the liquid he had transferred to a common flask or the spot at which he buried it.

They would find the empty vials in his pockets he brought to fill as promised.

His lie was successful, but his head still hurt and a part of him felt unclean. He remembered the words of Ophelia and that sustained him.

Unfortunately he was not allowed to immediately return to Poliska. The people he worked for were not convinced that this was the only building that contained such a miracle product. Two days later he met with his employer and over a drink they had a rather alarming discussion.

"Well Dagmar, I have a feeling that if we let you return this is the last we will see of you."

"What?"

"You have been unsuccessful in finding a new source…"

"A new source? This isn't a vein of gold! I can't just dig somewhere else Braydon."

"So you say."

Dagmar was speechless.

"You see, now that you no longer have this obligation you want to go home. But I feel there is something else at hand. And your task for us is not complete. When it is complete you may return."

Dagmar's heart sunk. Had he done the wrong thing? Should he just have extracted his private formula and one for them? He would be able to return then. Waiting would not work. There were no more like this. He'd be in Amira forever.

The thing that amazed him so would now become his private hell away from his love.

"No."

His counterpart smiled slightly.

"No, what, Dagmar?"

Dagmar shook his head from side to side and searched for words.

"No. This will not work. I must return. I will come back whenever you need me. But there are no other labs like this. You see, this was a special circumstance with a Saint…"

"Yes yes, a Saint nearby that has left. They do not leave."

The man leaned forward and became serious.

"My lord has not left in a Millenia. He is with us forever. This miracle formula is the final piece in his plans."

Dagmar drew his brows together and slowly sat up. The mere centimeters he added in distance from the man made him feel less threatened. Slightly. As Dagmar's heart sank even further he continued.

"You are part of a bigger plan, sir. We value what you can do for us. My lord values what you can do for him."

Dagmar responded meekly—like a mouse trapped in a corner listening to the cat pontificate about his rule over the entire house.

"But… but why? Why this?"

"Dagmar, in all these years the Saints have not been able to do what this potion can. Oh, there has been much talk, and we are all believers of course…"

He winked mid sentence.

"…but the lack of decay of certain items is just not enough. There are those of the people who grow restless. They want more. And even though it is hard for me to believe—fear is sometimes not enough."

"So…"

"So in front of hundreds of people my lord is going to heal someone very sick. And he is going to do it with the special potion you are going to find for me. And once that happens word will spread across all of Amira. And none of the other Saints will be able to duplicate this miracle. They will become lesser Saints or even false Saints in the eyes of their followers. There will finally be a leader."

The enormity of what was placed on the little man's shoulders was unbearable. Ophelia was wrong. He was not a good man. He worked for the most despicable people and they in turn worked for a Saint. And he was in the process of adding power to those who had too much power. He would aid in blinding the people. They would believe in magic because of Amiran Tec. It was the worst outcome imaginable and he would be at the root of it.

The man sat back in his chair.

"So you can see why we need you Dagmar. We believe in your skills. We believe in you. You're a good man."

Had he not felt so horrible Dagmar would have laughed out loud at the absurdity. He'd thrown his lot in for a chance at happiness for the rest of his life, and now he would have to stay on Amira to stumble on another miracle.

There was no way out of Amira except for the sailing ship these people controlled. Perhaps there was another way, but in all probability this was one of the only ships left. The powers that be had seized control of anything and anything they could. Any Amiran Tec that was preserved by a Saint would naturally be under the control of the Saint and his minions.

"Are you troubled?"

Dagmar came out of his wistful thoughts of Poliska. He blinked and answered.

"I am."

Terrified to say more he quickly became quiet. He shouldn't have even said those two words.

"Dagmar, you are a student of history. Your knowledge is great and perhaps there is no other with as much knowledge of the Old World—broken and limited as that is."

He had to admit that the man was correct. What Dagmar had seen and read had been fleeting and comprised mostly of disjointed bits of information. He had indeed seen the screens but they hadn't told him everything. There were various sciences, and histories of machines, and ways of life. So much could be learned but so little remained.

And something didn't quite add up. If he was right about the reach of the saints, even the obsessive hoarding wouldn't explain how little could be found. The cataclysm that turned the world upside down had destroyed so much and so many lives, but so much more should be left. It wasn't.

Perhaps he'd find out why. Perhaps he would be stuck here forever and never see Ophelia again. He could not even get a message to her… unless…

"And if I cannot find another source of this special formula?"

The man stroked his chin.

"Well then you will spend the rest of your life in good company, in the wondrous land of Amira."

Dagmar started to speak up and was cut off.

"In… our service of course."

If I could only get a message to Ophelia. Or... send for her? Would she even make the journey?

No, he could not involve her in this. He could not make her a captive like him.

He was between a rock and a rock and a hard place.

"Perhaps it is because you have so many distractions?"

"Pardon me?"

"Distractions. You love Amira yet you cannot wait to leave. So anxious. It makes no sense unless one considers possible distractions."

Dagmar's heart sunk. They knew.

His captor smiled.

"Rest up, friend Dagmar. My lord is patient. As long as we are in possession of this formula before the other Saints all is well, and it will be glorious."

"Will we not have to produce this on a regular basis?"

Dagmar thought of the hundreds and thousands who would flock to a city because of such a miracle healing. Countless had been led to believe they lived a longer life, that they were healed or that fortuitous things happened to them because of the influence of a Saint. But he knew the truth. An actual miracle healing would change the belief of everyone forever.

"Won't many come then, and expect the same?"

"My lord has asked for as much as was available, and then for the rest to be destroyed."

"What if someone else has had the same mission? What if that was exactly what happened—they collected all they could and then set fire to the building?"

The man considered his words. Dagmar was getting better at lying. The man looked at him suspiciously.

"What if that someone was you?"

He pointed his large finger at the smaller man.

"Me?"

"Yes. You speak wisely. If another Saint made the same deal with you… Then you provided the formula, and set fire to the building."

The man was half right which made Dagmar's breathing quite shallow.

He looked into Dagmar's eyes—hoping to find the guilt of the truth he'd just guessed. Dagmar swallowed.

The man saw the confusion and he pronounced Dagmar to be honest. He sat back and smiled a large grin. He laughed and placed his hands on the table.

"But of course you did not! No no. Relax. You are just as much the victim that we are. But you have made me consider that it is possible. At first I thought it to be a runaway fire, as you first suggested. But now…"

Dagmar's heart sunk even further.

"…now we must work faster, and race against the possibility. The Saints are separated by vast distance. The forces of one has never encroached upon the forces of another."

—

Dagmar's employers kept a very close watch on him. For a long time he did not feel safe returning to the spot at which he buried his prize. If someone stumbled across it they would think it is a flask of unknown black liquid but would not think it anything from the past. If his captors found it they would eventually figure out the truth. If they brought it to him he would have to choose between destroying it and preventing the tide of power from turning. But if he destroyed it he'd no longer have something very special to protect his dear Ophelia.

And all of his notes, transcriptions, records and scrolls had been seized by his employers. They said it was for safe keeping but he know it was a way to insure his loyalty. He would never abandon his lifetime of work, and if he did not possess it he could not sell it.

Fortunately for him, they were wrong.

He must escape, recover the flask, and somehow find passage on a ship that traveled to Poliska or at least the surrounding territories. His journey here was the result of a sailing ship that departed from the territories to the west of Poliska. And this was a very special circumstance. There was no such thing as a vessel making regular passage to and from his home country. Travel outside of Amira was strictly controlled by the Saints, or perhaps it was one Saint—he did not know. The men who he now thought of as captors were in charge of such a thing, and did not like operating the unusual ship. It was in disrepair and although it had been preserved, some damage had occurred over the years of operation. It limped back and forth. This may have been the last journey. Dagmar's thoughts and considerations made him feel even worse. Even his escape routes seemed futile. He could not even fully fathom what was happening.

He was numb, and would be for some time. In fact, much to his agony, he would languish in the coastal city of Amira for some time. Weeks became months, and months became years.

More than once he thought of simply telling his captors that he had started the fire. Perhaps they would kill him and end his pain. Or he would give up the vial and return to Ophelia without it, for empty handed was better than not at all.

He was still alive only due to his conviction that they would never let him go—he was simply too valuable. Even if he had delivered exactly what they'd asked for they would never let him go. They would also never let someone like him fall into the hands of another Saint. He was also too dangerous in the wild. What if he decided to start performing his own miracles? He would be a Bishop without a Saint.

Though he had continued to come across Amiran Tec, nothing was like the special Tec of the lab he watched go up in bright flames that night. He gained more knowledge as his captors grew more and more impatient until one day he was able to slip away.

He kept to the coastline in hopes of finding the sailing vessel or something like it. Modern vessels could not make the trip mostly due to legends that about sea monsters and the like. And Amirans in general believed their homeland was the only one in the world. To the Saints it was and that was perpetuated constantly—with the paradoxical exception of those that worked for them that knew better.

To find another Old World vessel was impossible. To find a modern one that had a captain willing to set sail for what was essentially a trip around the world to the other side of Amira was futile.

A chance encounter with a man with a sick child changed everything.

"Yes. Yessir, he is very sick. Are you a man of medicine? I live too far from the Saint to bring him and he cannot travel."

Dagmar took interest in the man. He looked so tired and old—probably a mirror for himself in his current state. He mentally prepared himself for the possibility of having to use the formula on his child. Perhaps at least some good would come of it.

As it turned out he was not in need of a miracle cure but just a simple elixir mixed by Dagmar. It was something that was common knowledge in the Old World but ignored now.

The man gained ten years of youth when his son got better and his happiness was infectious.

For the first time in years Dagmar smiled. When the drunken conversation ensued a few days later it was not the detailed rambling that made the difference, but Dagmar's repeated deflections and refusals to accept any form of payment from the poor man. Specifically, it was Dagmar's flippant request to which the man—so grateful to finally offer something of value for his son's life—replied:

"I have a boat."

The man was willing to brave the endless sea, the mystical sea monsters and even losing his life to transport Dagmar to this unknown land. Having just gained his son he was willing to never see him again. Such was the love of this parent. But this was different—if he perished at sea his son would still live and the man would have repaid a debt.

It took much time, preparation and explaining to make sure they had enough supplies. Dagmar used both a hand-written map as well as a very special little disk he cherished much—his compass.

Though the man thought they took too much food and supplies he obliged. Dagmar thought that any minute the man would back out of their deal having realized he made a deal with a madman that would lead him to his death trying to circumnavigate the entire world. In a few days they were on their way.

They did indeed have a difficult time reaching the shore of his homeland, but much to the man's surprise it did exist. As much as he asserted they had simply sailed to the other side of Amira, Dagmar thought he convinced him otherwise. He and Dagmar found a place to stay, and in a short while was on his way back to his home. Dagmar wished him well and provided him with a trinket of the Old World to help him once again find home.

He hoped that the man would now live a long and happy life with his healthy son.

The elation building in him was equal to the dread. He was back in Poliska with his vial. The years had been unimaginably difficult. Day after day he cursed his life—for every day he was in Amira he was not with Ophelia. His imagination filled his mind with what he could be doing with her on any given day—holding hands, taking countless walks, enjoying the picnics she grew to love so much. He would have already asked her to marry him. He sometimes heard the voices of their children laughing as he fell asleep some nights. The image of her eyes and the sunlight on her hair were as vivid in his mind as if he'd seen her yesterday. To see her smile outside of just his imagination would be more than anything life could offer him.

He was exhausted, numb, distraught and empty. But now the unsurmountable had been accomplished. Though he could never get those days back he would start anew with her. There was only one step left.

After a few weeks travel he would accomplish the last step. Unfortunately this last step came to him in the form of a letter that was left for him with Ophelia's parents.

Dear Dagmar -

I have waited so long for you. I knew in my heart that when you left me that you would not return. I shed so many tears for you but now understand it was not meant to be. I have found a man that has some wealth and is not subject to flights of fancy.

I am sorry that I cannot be what you want, need and deserve.

I love you.

- Lia

Dagmar died a thousand deaths that day.

With each word he read some of his soul escaped his body like wisps of vapor from a hot cup of tea. It left him and spread to the ether. It was who he was and what he would be. It was all the goodness he believed he had within him because of her. It was invisible yet tangible; hidden yet apparent. It expanded to the infinite from a space he held within himself that was only slightly smaller than that.

And he could feel it. All the warmth was escaping and there was nothing he could do about it but helplessly watch and feel it leave. As time no longer had meaning in an amount of time somewhere between seconds and an eternity it was gone. There would be no night and day; no darkness and light—just the cold grey of existence.

He now felt the numbness and the emptiness.

Dagmar reckoned he had waited, believed and traveled more than any human in the entire world. His sole focus had been her and he had done the impossible to return. His heart was open and had made a grand and great place for her. Up until that moment it still contained the love and the memory he had of her, and only wished for it to be refilled again. But it would not. It would never be.

In his pocket he carried the futile reminder of the reason he left, the reason he returned and the reason he failed.

And now he had nothing.

THE BISHOP AND A METHOD

"Sit. Sit and drink and talk."

The thin man held everything close to himself as he sat. He looked around repeatedly and his partner was exceptionally friendly. It confused him as he was the buyer and the man was the seller. Why be so engaging when you are already at an advantage? Instead the seller was as nice as possible—even generous with drinks. At last the older man spoke.

"I am sitting. Why do you want to meet in person? How does that suit you?"

"Relax…"

He spread his thick hands and responded.

"It's just a drink. We have much to talk about."

He raised his glass and smiled a very convincing smile—the kind an alligator might before swallowing a bird whole.

"I have seen many things…"

He sipped his drink as the one in purple eyed him up and down. When it was obvious the older man was just going to suspiciously stare at him he put his drink down and pressed further.

"Oh please! Drink, Bishop. Yes yes, I know. Don't act so surprised. I know all about you and your… desire."

His enthusiasm to calm his buyer down had an undesired effect but he would ride it out. His property was priceless and the man would probably pay anything. He just continued to smile and wait. Finally the older man drank his drink.

"Ahh. That's better. We have no quarrel. We are alike, no? You and I seek the same things."

Before the man could object to such an absurd statement he continued. He would not lose ground—or this sale.

"I have something to show you. I will prove to you that not only do I possess the means to garner what you desire, but I will also prove that I have experienced it."

The older man tilted his head as if looking at a lame animal he would put down. He said one word with much distaste. It was meant as a question.

"IT."

The heavy man slammed his drink down. And then laughed.

"Ha ha! Yes. *It*."

He leaned it closely, conspiratorially, as if he was about to speak blasphemy.

"Amiran Tec."

The other man's eyes narrowed and the fat man continued.

"Oh, not just any Amiran Tec. It is a *conveyance*. The very thing that will bring what you desire to you. This is no book, no trinket and no small shiny apparatus. This is something that…"

"The conveyance…"

The older man was now entranced. He was mesmerized by the word. He said it again.

"The conveyance… you possess the conveyance…?"

After a long pause in which many options were weighed the man answered.

"You know of what I speak. Yes. So few know of this secret. It is a millennium-old secret. It is the most complex thing that has survived the Old World. And it has survived because of the very thing you seek!"

He paused for some time and drank his drink. He eventually continued.

"Well, I do not possess it. My employers do, but I am free to use it. And I am free to use to to convey what you seek.

He stared at the man. He would speak last.

"You will retrieve it for me? You know where it is?"

The fat man smiled. The deal was done. He was rich.

"And—dear Lucjan—only I have the means to bring it to Poliska."

A SAINT AWAKENS

The man in purple robes clutched a staff in one hand and in the other held a a scroll. He read from the scroll again and again. The words were nonsense but he spoke them aloud as best he could. He had invested a fortune in obtaining it and the statue. The means of conveyance was nothing short of magical, and just finding it had proven he was on the right track. The conveyance was nothing compared to what he could do.

With everything in place he was ready. He would have the power of the Saints and Amiran magic would make it obey. In fact he would have a power even greater for he would have control over all of them with what he now possessed. He cleared his throat and took a deep breath. All of the learning and the reading and the scrolls lead up to this. If he was right he would unleash this power for himself and it would do his bidding. It was trapped in a way that it could not free itself. It could not use its vast power directly against him. It had been awakened after almost one thousand years of slumber, and he had taken it while it slept. He would learn of how. He would have all of his questions answered. He practically shook with excitement and anticipation. If what he read was true this was the most powerful Saint.

At last he spoke to it—nay—he commanded it.

"Arise!"

The scroll was key in his incantations. It was covered in hand-written symbols and had been translated from old Amiran texts. The person who had done it was clearly brilliant and possibly a Bishop such has himself. It spoke of the sciences of the day and the workings of the

Saints. It even touched on how they were originally summoned. The person had used modern day tools to create a means to understand the workings of not only Amira but of the Saints themselves. It was unlike anything Lucjan had ever experienced. He almost believed another Saint worked with his Bishop to create such elaborate and intimate plans.

The transcriber was very specific in stating that it all made sense, and that it was all part of a learnable science. He had much passion in the matter but he did not understand magic, or mystery, or the unknown. He spent too much time attempting to break things down into mundane information.

The general populace didn't have time or effort to learn the minutia. The average person did not want to know—they instead wanted to be led. They wanted to believe that there was always something more powerful, more mystical and more wondrous than anything they could comprehend. Then they would turn off their brain and obey. To be enthralled and to serve was their natural way.

Lucjan had learned the same lesson the Saints learned a thousand years ago.

Today the self-proclaimed Bishop would learn the dutifully transcribed and translated scrolls to create a special environment to not only support the thing he had in his possession, but to also contain it. He would have power over the most powerful thing in the world and it would do his bidding.

He alone would command the most powerful of all the Saints.

And he was about to awaken it from its self-induced slumber.

He said it again.

"Arise. I have awakened you and you are bound."

When the thing did awaken it was magnificent. It was large and very heavy and it had taken much to bring it into his hidden building. Soon he would move it to a place that it belonged—a church. But he would need its powerful magic to move it. It barely fit on the conveyance and moving it to even this location took special construction and reinforced carts.

At last it spoke, and its voice was just like those had described it, yet this was different. The demeanor was one that he could not discern. Was it hurt? Or damaged? Was it half-awake?

It was indescribable. He was terrified. Had it not been for the seemingly soft demeanor of it he would have probably run from the room.

It was disoriented. It was not unfriendly but clearly did not like the predicament it had been placed in. The thing had a surprising understanding of the past, and Amrian Tec. Many moments were spent as it seemed to almost be in shock, as if it was reading from hundreds of books at the same time.

He stared at it as it slowly became fully awake. At no time did it make any sudden movements that frightened him but he was still weary. The conditions that held it into place were simple and apparently effective. He alone had the wherewithal to perform such a thing.

He pondered. Well, perhaps the one that could perform it—the one that had created the texts, but his whereabouts were unknown.

He grimaced at the thought. No, only Lucjan had not only the means but the will to do such a thing. Yes!

He found quite quickly that the Saint had powers beyond what had been recorded through history. Did they all have this power? If so, why wouldn't they use it? This Saint had powers that truly were magical despite what the texts said.

What surprised him more than anything was the knowledge he learned about the inner workings of the Saints themselves. These were hidden things that no man or woman had ever been privy to.

He became more and more excited as he conversed with it. He decided that he would keep the sessions short. Perhaps prolonged interaction would strengthen it to the point that it could escape.

Unlike what the myths told, this one had not been banished by the others but instead had hidden away of its own accord. And that was when he understood—it had done so because it kept its power to itself. To sleep was to deprive the other saints of it.

Even in hibernation it still affected the surrounding area. Because of this the conveyance survived all of these years, but like so many bits of Amiran Tec enjoying it was fleeting, for the things still required upkeep.

And in some cases like an oil lamp, some of the things required fuel.

So much to learn. So much power to be had.

As the days went on he was able to move it to a location he'd held for some time. It was a building but only a hundred years or so ago and it was made to look like a building of the Old World—the kind that had been razed so long ago. It would be his church, he would be the Bishop and this was his Saint.

Unlike the others, in this case he would be in charge.

In his mind he saw no scenario in which his power wouldn't grow to encompass all of Poliska and the outer territories. And with his newfound knowledge of Amira there was no limit to what he could do.

It was as if one day an ant had wandered from the ant hill and captured a soldier equipped with both sword and torch. The other ants would not stand a chance—especially if there was only one such soldier in the entire would.

And in his case there was. He was a very excited and powerful ant this day.

Nothing stood in his way. For weeks he conversed, learned and planned. His was very close to taking action when the Saint spoke a prediction of its own.

In a matter of days Lucjan would be dead.

LETTERS

The box was metal and looked like nothing he had ever seen. It was crafted with perfection. He admired the hinges and the cover. He had seen a finely crafted timepiece and he imagined that a clockmaker would be required for such precision. This he promptly brought to his lord.

"Read it to me."

"But, there are many. Is it a book of some sort? All of them? Perhaps you would like to…"

"I said read them to me."

With that the young man sat down at the altar and begin to read the letters that were hand written. One by one he read them to the expressionless face of the statue. It was an honor to impart the knowledge. Perhaps it was a test. Sometimes a word made no sense. Having learned reading in such a limited capacity it appeared this was from a slightly different language.

July 22nd, 2050

Dear sis,

It's been a few weeks and since the sunlight isn't going away i thought I'd write you. I've been on a farm. i know there's no mail service but I'm writing this for two reasons I suppose—to make sure you know what I've been doing and to just stay sane.

I have to hope and believe that you're OK too. I know we're both 1,000's of miles from mom but if there's any way to reach her I know you are trying.

I'm with someone who is very bright and in fact she knows a lot about what's going on.

I'll write more later as I know. I do this for a living but now can't find the words. Just thought I'd say hi. Maybe this will be the only letter I write. With my luck a helicopter will come and I'll get to tell you this myself and the drinks are probably on you.

Love you.

- Marty

Oct, 2050

Dear sis,

A lot has happened. I'm sure you know. The aurora borealis has been so beautiful, and even better than the ones we saw on the Alaska trip. I'm sure you know. NY is closer to the pole.

Though we had ample supplies we've always been concerned with looters. Even the best people can be desperate and we've seen a lot of them.

We knew we would have to eventually move. See, Nik is pretty smart. You'd like her. She kicks my ass and I think she might even be smarter than me. I know. I know.

The weather has been so weird.

I'm not sure what day it is though she marks a calendar. I guess I'm in denial about how much time is passing. So to me its just October. No halloween though, but I did make a ghost out of a tissue.

Anyway stay safe, please. I love you.

- Marty

Feb 2051

Dear sis -

I'm sure glad I'm stuck in Texas. The winter in the north would not be easy. I have bad news. It looks like some people found out about our secret farm. We had to defend ourselves. I've never killed anyone until now. It was not something i ever want to do again. This is all just wrong and I wish every night that we can go back to normal. I cried. I cried a lot. I cry about you, and about mom. I cry about the people that have died and now i cry about the ones I've killed.

You know, all the stuff I used to write about is so trivial compared to just surviving. I was so stupid. We all were. The stuff we thought was important wasn't.

I went out back into the city and its not something I'd ever imagine. In such a short while everything is just toppled. Nik says the lightning caused a lot of damage but I think the crowds just finished the job. There was almost no one there and we think they went to farms like us, or already lived there. There's a lot of animals.

I really really hope you're alright. We talked about maybe making a pilgrimage but Nik things the best place would be south and not north because of the winters.

We are going to stay here as long as we can, but I don't know what will happen if they come for us again.

March 2051

Dear sis -

I know I've mentioned Nik a few times but I have to tell you that I'm very much in love with her. Your brother is cohabitation with a woman you've never met. I know. I can just hear you yelling at me and asking lots of questions.

God I wish I could hear your voice again, even if it was a call or a message or something. She has given me so much to live for and she is... just.. If stuff was working you'd see her on the news I suppose. But then if stuff was working i never would have ended up here.

She makes my head and my heart hurt and I've never talked with someone so much. Sometimes we talk through the night and forget to go to sleep. Though she say's I've taught her things she amazes me any just how many skills she has. The thing about her is that everything she does she just... well, she's the best.

God I hope you're ok. I really want to see you, and i want you to meet her. She say's she'd love to meet you but I know in my heart she knows. She knows what i know.

I will miss you so much.

Love,

- Marty

June 2051

Dear sis -

I was thinking of writing you monthly but i only have so much paper and i have no idea how long these pens will last. I mean, i don't even write on paper usually. I bet any stationary left has been used for firewood.

So i guess I'm just going to write you when something happens, which it has. Things have been awfully quiet so we took a risk and both traveled out. We took our bikes. Did I tell you that we both have the slickest bikes? Anyway we went out and we couldn't find anyone. Nik thinks we lost a lot of the population. She thinks as much as 70% or maybe a lot more. Probably more she says but i can't imagine more than half. half is an easy number right? Thats just too many. So she thinks with all those people unable to make it due to lack of drugs, medical attention, and food and so forth that well that's it.

Yeah, that's it.

Wait. We went out again—it's later. It's been like a month, sorry, I didn't start a new sheet.

We met a group of people who were like nomads. Nik says they were smart. We actually did a little trade with them. Seems like the people who were the preppers had a better chance of surviving, but these were just smart people who got lucky. i guess like me. Nik thinks its a genetic thing that the northern lights signaled some bad stuff coming down. I was dumb and just looked at them and she said we are just lucky because our genetics were hardy and that is probably who is left... The healthy people. The people who could take care of themselves. And the hardy ones.

Natural selection. I guess that means you're still out there maybe? After all you're my sis.

OK. I'm done on this one. I love you.

- Your bro

August 2051

Dear sis -

I'm going to be a dad. I bet you are wondering why we would bring a child into the world. I wondered the same thing. You and i used to argue about over population but now its the opposite. It was sort of our duty. Don't get me wrong. We did this out of love and it just felt right. We are in a good place to take care of the baby. We are both nervous but nik tells me she's got great child-bearing hips. Seriously she said that. She talks like that. I told you that you'd like her. I have to be honest and tell you I'm terrified. I take so much for granted with deliveries of babies. Its like humans aren't even ready and we have them too early. I'm scared. I really am, but I can't get over how happy we both are. I sound crazy. maybe this is the wrong thing. I gotta believe its right. Its the only right we have together. Sort if making it up as we go on, you know? Its probably what everyone is doing now. At least the ones that are left. I hope you're one of those.

I love you.

- Marty

November 2051

Dear sis -

It's going to happen any day. We can't see the northern lights any more. Nik says that's a good thing and that we are probably protected again. That means the baby won't be at risk and can go outside, but it will probably be hardy like us anyway.

You know I miss music. I miss a lot of things I suppose. I miss you. i miss riding in planes. I mis spending too much money on dinner. I miss having a lot more clothing choices. I don't miss being in constant contact with everyone including the people I don't want to be connected to. its really made me value the connections I have. Right now that's just you and Nik and the baby.

OMG.

I know unlike me you're the praying type so pray for a safe delivery. We have done everything we can to prepare for it. Ive run the perimeter every single day to make sure no one is near us. I don't want any stragglers or visitors when it happens. Nik said her mom had a natural birth with her, just like mom did with us. So I'm hopeful.

I don't want to lose her or both of them. I've been so lucky to have found her.

I promise you that I will be the best dad i can be and we will teach it everything it needs to grown up strong, and smart. I swear I will do this if everything goes OK. Promise me if you're out there that you're praying for us. I don't know what

I'll do if something goes wrong.

I miss you so much and wish I could see your face. All the pics I had of you were in the cloud and on my screen.

Love you,

\- Marty

March, 2052

Dear sis,

I'm sorry I haven't written. We have been so busy with the baby. It did happen a few days after I last wrote you. Things were scary and I think it was a contest to see which one of us was the most scared. But everything was OK. She made us forget about the world.

She's beautiful. She's a perfect little girl. When I heard her cry it was new life. I don't know how much new life is around any more but she gives us both hope.

OK, I'm hoping you can read this. I'm sorry for the tears and spots on the page and I can't spare another. I've never been so happy and I know that sounds so selfish but I can't help it. You always said I'd probably be first even though you're the big sister. Sorry I beat you. Maybe I didn't?

I wish I could send you a pic but I wouldn't have had it any other way than to just be there in the moment. Even if I could. Listen to me. Ha.

We argued about the name a few times but honestly I just wanted her to be healthy. She is.

In the end Nik thought it best that we name her after you. The concession was that we would give your name a Russian flair.

So, you're an aunt. Congratulations, sis.

I love you Anne and I hope some day you can see her.

"Enough" The Saint had waved his hand. His attendant did not look up. He was afraid and ashamed. The tears running down Andrew's cheeks would not be appreciated by his lord. It was a great honor to be asked to read something to him and it should be done with precision. The book had a thin loop of metal that curled over and over again. The metal wire was thread through holes in the yellow parchment and more than one page almost folded at the top in which the tiniest of folds were present. Upon examination they were very tiny holes. At each end of a page he was able to pull the page over itself and sweep it to the back of the book. Andrew had never seen a book that was bound on the top instead of the side and this one was bound delicately with metal. It was almost as if it was intended that you take a page out easily. He thought it an amazing bit of Amiran Tec but of odd design. There were no page numbers and the front cover was of a harder material and bore a seal that he did not recognize. Next to the seal it read "American Technology"

Fortunately it had survived in perfect condition but he did not know just how old it was. If it was Amiran Tec then he believed it was from a time before the Saints. The words and numbers might denote the time or perhaps the day, but they mentioned nothing of the year of All Saints. If true then the book was from over five hundred years ago for now it was 999 in the Year of All Saints. This book was from year zero. He realized how valuable this was just then. If true it was a history of the coming of the Saints and the experiences of common people. He doubted his lord would allow him to take it from the church and show others and the punishment for sneaking it out would be more than severe. Perhaps some day, or perhaps during a sermon they could read from it—and learn. So little was known of history that wasn't told directly by the Saints, and they were never allowed to write it down.

He wasn't even a third done with the book when the Saint interrupted him. The story intrigued him. The man was chronicling his life to his sister. It was a beautiful story and perhaps fiction. He wanted to continue reading and find out what happened. Would the little girl grow up? Would the man ever find his sister? He mentioned locations that Andrew had not heard of, but perhaps they were located in the Old World.

The Saint took the book from him and held it in his hand. The light of the fireplace flickered on his grey face as he was expressionless. Had the story not touched him? There was so much more to read.

Andrew would do everything he could to make sure he was the one to read the rest of it to the Saint. He could convince his lord to let him read it in private to make sure he pronounced all of the words correctly. Then he could read it aloud to him when it was perfect. He wanted to impress him. He had seen other books, but those were in a special print that could not be reproduced now. This however was hand-written.

Excited now he blinked and looked up.

"*No…*"

It was barely perceptible. The word came out of Andrew's mouth as the flames engulfed the book. It was quite flammable and even the cover took flame easily. It tumbled further behind the top log as he stared at the menacing orange and reds.

Andrew looked back at the Saint.

It smiled.

"You have read enough."

He glanced back and forth between the fire and the Saint.

"Oh, and if you speak of this to anyone it will mean your death. Mark my words, Andrew."

It chilled him to the bone and indeed he marked those words. He would never speak of the book again and it was devastating. He fought tears again. So much history lost. It clarified what other had only whispered about.

Though the Saint had taken this precious artifact from him he'd given him something he never had before.

Hope.

AFTERWARD

This one was hard. That is not to say that it was difficult to write. It developed like the duet. But in writing this prequel I knew what *was* to happen and it wasn't pleasant. There was no happy ending and I am someone who needs a happy ending. As it was the prelude to the events of *The Sword and the Sunflower* and *Amira*, I knew the story would have to be told.

I couldn't imagine telling this story while I was writing those books—it was too terrible. What I had was the aftermath and the hero's journey moving forward based on the wonderful poem that came to me after a walk.

But this was different. It was a showcase for how the world had evolved though a thousand years and over thirty generations.

I chose not to reveal much of how the government and the military responded. Most apocalyptic stories immediately show the government's response—typically to enforce how bad things are—because we tend to think of the military as the best we can do, the end-all be-all.

With everyone cut off from other countries I chose to show a more intimate, character-driven story of what they experienced.

It is absolutely amazing how much we depend on out technology. The Carrington event is real. The flipping of the poles is real and really does happen (we think) every 200-300k years. We are fortunate (maybe more than we know) to live on a planet with a very powerful magnetic field. It protects us like a force field and without it life may never have evolved. When it is missing (Mars does not have one) it's a tangible stumbling block for establishing a foothold on other planets.

Thirty generations is an awful lot of generations. Most people don't have a connection to their great-grandparents—that's only three generations removed. Imagine ten times that many. Their lives and lifestyles are so far removed as to feel alien.

This time there was no music. While Ludovico and others guided and provided a backdrop for me, this was written without any themes.

In this book I considered telling the story out of order, but a chronology seemed like the worst choice for mixing up the timeline. The beginning of Martin and Nikola's relationship seemed like it would have made a good starting point. It would have been a bit confusing to skip ahead in a story such as this, however.

In all of the tragedy, it turned out I had written a series of love stories, and that made me smile. Even in the face of destruction, cataclysm and change one thing always appears—love. Sometimes it is triumphant. Sometimes it is not.

So I hope you enjoyed the one thousand year history of the Saints. A book such as this can only contain so much and three hundred or so pages is only so much to work with. More importantly is the respect to your attention span. I hope I kept it, held it and returned it to you intact.

GLOSSARY OF AMIRAN TEC

In case you are curious as to some of the technology mentioned in this book, here is a bit more information. One does not need to read this to understand their place in the story but it is included for those that want or need to know more.

Medi-Band: The medi-band is a small, watch-like device that originated from the various fitness bands. The technology allows it to sense far more than what the old bands could. Not only are the clever sensors able to report more and more accurate information, but the device has the ability to communicate with implants if the user has them. Having an implant became as common as wearing a fitness band of old and many enjoyed the benefits of this monitoring while others were troubled by the lack of confidentiality of data as it was stored in the cloud. In addition to monitoring, various drugs can be dispensed though high pressure injectors located in the contact area. Though not much space is available within, it is large enough for a dose or two, or microdoses of enhancing drugs and even vitamins. The bands also allow the application of drugs when not normally possible in the home - e.g. the ingestion of meds when the patient is in deep sleep (when certain liver functions are at their peak). This would be impossible other than in a 24 hour patient care facility.

Hyper-Bike: Like the "hover boards" of our time this name is misleading. Just as the hover boards don't actually hover but are instead a small stand with (typically) two wheels, so are the hyper-bikes not hyper-fast transport. Instead they are bikes built from the ground up with large scale electric motors built not into the hub but the wheels themselves. These large flat disc motors utilize the great advantage of torque as well as regenerative breaking that are used when needed. Unlike motorized bikes from our time they have a range that makes them incomparable to anything we can currently devise. Our electric bikes have a very short range and the battery and motors add so much weight as to make riding them as normal bikes difficult. Not so for these bikes. It would be hard for someone of our time to actually tell the difference between a standard hybrid bike and a hyper-bike.

The Hyper-bikes became very popular and at one point outnumbered actual manual, non-powered bikes.

2050 & Energy: 2050 saw the mass adoption of electrical vehicles with fossil fuel vehicles being an oddity. Fossil fuel companies had already become 'energy' companies and all but one really focused on the sustainable production of energy. What they did not do was focus on the storage of said energy which was an element of the equation. To solve the equation one must address the impact of production of the energy, the storage and implementation of the energy and the disposal of the storage devices (the batteries). It is one thing to create an electric car, but if you destroy the environment in both production of energy and disposal of batteries you have solved nothing.

Solarization had also been quite prevalent, but again this was just a means to produce energy (in a rather inefficient manner until recently). The energy still needs to be stored and regulated. And solar panels were also very impactful to the environment.

Nikola Tesic solved the equation. The production of energy cost nothing to the environment. The storage was non existent as there was no real battery. The devices converted, used and throttled the energy as it came though. And since there was no battery there was nothing to dispose of. Only the technology that contained and converted would eventually need to be disposed of, and that could last decades before even needing adjustment.

2050 & Transportation: No real paradigm shift occurred in public and mass transportation. However the idea of self-driving cars continued to be adopted and embraced by the public. This meant that the number of cars on the road increased and rather than plan cities around central transportation, they were adapted with enhanced roads making it easier for the car's AI to navigate. Pedestrians became more mindful of cars, as they couldn't count on the drivers to notice them if the suddenly appeared in a crosswalk when they had no desire to make eye contact on a bad day. It also saw the inclusion of smart stop signals that communicated with the automation of cars. These lights adapted to the live traffic flow. Cars would no longer have to wait at a red light with no traffic present from perpendicular directions. In addition, the regulation and abundance of these cars made for proper schools of vehicles. Like the fish groupings they were named after, these groups of cars could travel as a pack in large numbers when their destinations were in alignment. It was quite common for the same cars to join a school together on the way to work each day, with the occupants viewing this time as a group meeting to play a game or chat. A number of book clubs utilized these schools as their primary time to meet in their busy lives. Again it was this freedom and control that caused the numbers of private vehicles to increase and not do the opposite.

Air-taser: Similar to the tasers of today, the gun delivers a specialized electric shock to the victim. However, in place of physical hooks that are shot out and attached to thin wires, the device relies on something else: lasers. The mouth of the device produces multiple, extremely thin laser beams. The beams are strong enough to ionize the air thins turning the air into a conductive material. The first such guns used only two lasers, but are now typically produced with groups of eight with emitters thus making it much easier to complete a circuit and stun your victim. The strength of these lasers can present an additional hazard but it was deems that this hazard was no worse that that presented by the sharp hooks. The device only proceeds these beams for short bursts to minimize the danger. Like the hooks of old they can complete the circuit through thin material but are fairly useless against think clothing. The Law Enforcement Reorganization act of 2028 paved the way for non-lethal weapons being the default for officers in the U.SA.

Solarization: The mass adoption of solarization happened due to a perfect storm of occurrences. Well known companies were now mass-producing them, solar efficiency broke the elusive 50% milestone outside of the lab (current panels are only 20% efficient at best), battery storage density had a few breakthroughs, their integration into everything from roofs to the exterior of vehicles (including aircraft) and the commonality of electric aircraft. Of all the energy collection options solar had the goodwill favor of the public, and the last roadblock (lack of noxious elements that did not bode well for disposal) was removed thanks to American Technology. Solarization and battery storage density pushed each other in a never-ending loop of cost, efficiency integration into every day life.

2050 & Nanite technology: 2050 saw the first true experimental tiny particle machines in use. Unlike what had been previously portrayed in the media they did not take the form of extremely complicated insect-like machines. Instead, the cusp of technology could only produce what amounted to be tiny sphere-like devices with propulsion, communication and manipulation. The first use of such a substance was in the repair and alteration of living bodies. Such devices lacked the strength and manipulation ability to affect any real change in substantive structures. They could not combine and build ad-hoc devices. The softness of living tissue as well as the fluid pathways made for the ideal starting point. The human body produced not only heat but a weak electrical field that could be utilized for power. Operating in any other environment for any other task proved to be a challenge that was as yet to be met. Even in 2050 the technology was in its infancy.

2050 in general: Technology does not quite move at the speed we think and hope it does. Understand that the vast majority of the world is driven by wealth, power and above all stability of the ruling class. Game-changing technologies come and go and are absorbed into the power structure. The patent system in the United States is such that it squelches most incremental ideas. Large corporations squat upon patents that would change the world. it is not uncommon for them to spend a fortune in constant lobbying to hold and even extend they laws, and that even includes something less impactful as copyrights.

Flying cars are never going to arrive. The literal added dimension of flying cars can only be handled one way—logically and properly, and no one is thinking in those terms. They just want to see The Jetsons. Personal transportation is not going to yield to mass transportation unless a culture allows it. However, using personal transportation *as* mass transit is an easy possibility (see *2050 and transportation* above).

We are never going to see real holograms until we see force fields. And we are never going to see the latter until we have a new understanding of energy. When we do, it will fundamentally change the way we interact with technology. Until then we will have our precious screens. But after, they will be as laughable as picture tube TVs.

IMHO, of course.

ABOUT THE AUTHOR

Mark Bradford produces and hosts a weekly podcast about Time, Energy and Resources that also features interviews with amazing people. Listen to ***The Alchemy for Life*** podcast for more insight, on iTunes and most other podcast providers. Subscribe and you won't miss them.

www.alchemyfor.life

Mark produces ***The Status Game*** series of books and card game that helps demonstrate, educate and enlighten people about an invisible but very real aspect on how we connect, and what we like.

His answers have over two million answer views on Quora - a question and answer community.

Follow Mark on Instagram for announcements and things related to his content - books, podcasts, etc.

@authormarkbradford

It's a fun feed with daily posts. Have a question? Ask it on the podcast.

Have a book club? You can usually find book club questions for his books on his web site for all endeavors:

markbradford.org

Books by Mark Bradford

The Status Game
The original book on status and online dating.

The Status Game II
How status is the key to all relationships - business and personal.

OneSelf
Faith of a simpler, more direct kind. Or just nonsense.

Alchemy for Life
Everything you need to know about Life Coaching in one book. And 16 formulas for success.

The Sword and the Sunflower trilogy:

The Sword and the Sunflower

Amira

Upside Down

Coming soon:

Discover Your Gages
The workbook companion to The Status Game II.

?

If you liked this book
I would appreciate it if you took a minute
to review it.